BOOKS BY SHELBY HEARON

Afternoon of a Faun   1983
Painted Dresses   1981
Barbara Jordan: A Self-Portrait   1979
(with Barbara Jordan)
A Prince of a Fellow   1978
Now and Another Time   1976
Hannah's House   1975
The Second Dune   1973
Armadillo in the Grass   1968

*Afternoon
of a Faun*

AFTERNOON
OF A FAUN

Shelby Hearon

Atheneum 1983 New York

I wish to thank the John Simon Guggenheim Memorial Foundation for its support.

Library of Congress Cataloging in Publication Data

Hearon, Shelby, ——
Afternoon of a faun.
I. Title.
PS3558.E256A69   1983   813'.54   82-16301
ISBN 0-689-11350-1

Published simultaneously in Canada by McClelland & Stewart Ltd.
Composed by Maryland Linotype Composition Company,
  Baltimore, Maryland
Printed and bound by Fairfield Graphics, Fairfield, Pennsylvania
Designed by Mary Cregan
First Edition

FOR BILL,
my family

CONTENTS

Was it a dream I loved?

MALLARMÉ

I

Jeanetta

T H E mirrors were wonderful. You could really see your-self.

She didn't know how her mom knew how much she wanted mirrors. She'd thrown her arms around her mom and hugged her about five times and even jumped up and down she was so excited. She guessed it was because they were so close that her mom always knew what was on her mind.

They had been a complete surprise; she had thought that her bedroom was all finished when they hung the café curtains. She'd screamed and hugged her mom when she got home this afternoon and saw them. It was the most wonderful thing, because she had always wanted to have them, but she hadn't even let herself think that you could have them at home.

The mirrors were the kind that you pulled the back off and then stuck in place, and they were on all four walls, making each wall look like it was solid mirror. There was a three-foot row of mirror tiles everywhere except where the windows were, and the draped valences over the bed (the mix of yellow and pink checks that her mom had swagged to look like the head of a four-poster).

She'd gone to school in her pink sweater and pale yellow skirt that had just a thin line of pink in the plaid. It was her favorite outfit, and she'd saved it to wear for her birthday.

Those were her two favorite colors, pink and pale yellow, and most people couldn't see them as going together, but she did. She'd had the skirt made, to be able to find something with the two colors in it. Her mom had said she could do her room over for her birthday, the whole room in pale yellow and pink, and she had got to pick everything out. They found a tiny pink and white check which they made into dust ruffles and pillow shams, and the same tiny check in yellow and white which they quilted into a bedspread and ruffled into a skirt for the vanity. And at the windows they put double café curtains, pink check at the top and yellow check at the bottom. It was perfect, and really different. Everybody she knew, even her best friend Leslie, had a blue room or a light green room; nobody thought to mix pink and yellow. She and her mom had finished it last weekend; and she was going to have a slumber party in the spring, when it got warmer, to show everybody.

She used to imagine herself in front of mirrors like this whenever she got dressed, wondering if the mirrors would show herself the way she thought she looked, or if they would lie. She would turn around and around, imagining mirrors all over, the way they were when you went shopping and you could see yourself from every angle, and you would wonder if the image you saw was the same image other people saw when they looked at you, and usually you could be confident it was. Shopping excited her, because of that facet of it.

Now she had that at home.

4

She liked most the fact that you could keep looking forever and still not catch your expression exactly. Having them in your own room was even more private than in the store shopping, because if someone was with you, Leslie or the clerk or your mom, you couldn't stand looking at yourself the whole time; they would think you were stuck on yourself, and that wasn't it at all. You weren't admiring what you saw, but trying to be sure that what you saw was how you really looked.

Today wasn't actually her birthday; it was tomorrow. But that was Saturday, and she liked to celebrate with her friends. She had always considered it special to be born on Valentine's Day, because the whole school had a party with you. When she was little she would come home with two cards from everybody; that was fun, coming home all excited and loaded down. That was back in grade school but she still remembered getting all those cards. She used to string them up around her room and leave them until summer.

David had walked her home today the way he did every day, and they had talked about tonight. They were going out to dinner, he'd picked out a place but he hadn't told her where, and then they were supposed to go to a movie. His father was going to bring them home; but except for that they would be by themselves all evening. Daddy and her mom had promised her that when she was fifteen she could single-date. And they had kept their word. She was lucky in that respect; not everybody had parents like hers.

Jeanetta had to admit that she was not completely in love with David. It made her ashamed, as she was supposed to be. She hadn't even told her mom, and she didn't keep things from her mom ever. Her mom even knew the first time she had kissed David, and everything. Whenever they went out, she and David—double-dating with Pam and Jeff, who weren't their best friends, but Jeff was old enough to drive, and Pam's mom knew Daddy and her mom—she would come back and tell her mom all about it. Her mom would be in the kitchen, and have hot chocolate ready, with marshmallows, and they would talk a long time about what a good time Jeanetta had had.

She thought she might be going to break up with David because in three months he would be able to drive, and then they would have permission to go out by themselves two nights a weekend, and she knew what David wanted to happen then. Because he had said. Already he had got her to promise that for her birthday she would take her sweater off and let him look at her breasts. She had said yes because he said he loved her, and because she didn't want to hurt him, and he'd been her boyfriend for a long time. Besides, she wanted to let him look, just once, anyway.

Sometimes lately she felt like crying and she didn't know why. After she'd been out with David and Pam and Jeff, and they'd gone to a movie, or had a lot of fun, and then she'd let him kiss her a lot in the car, she'd feel like that. It was dumb, but you couldn't help it. She'd asked Leslie about it, and Leslie had said that meant she wasn't really in love with David. Which was part of how she knew for sure.

He wasn't coming until seven o'clock tonight, because Daddy wanted to see her a little while first. Tomorrow, her real birthday, she would spend the night with Leslie, and because the Jay-Teens weren't supposed to go to the School for the Deaf until the next Saturday, she would have the whole day to just enjoy it being her birthday and to appreciate her mirrors. In a way she missed stringing the Valentine cards all over her room, and the birthday parties you had in those days where the whole class came and there were favors and prizes, and candles to blow out. But she was too grown-up for that now.

Daddy was pretending that he would get his feelings hurt if she went out on a date with David before he got home from his office. She knew he was just pretending, because he liked David and bragged about him a lot. He thought David was special, because he was good-looking and made good grades and came from a nice family. Sometimes she thought Daddy liked David better than she did, but then he and David could talk about the same things, because he was a boy. She knew Daddy felt relief that she hadn't brought home someone that he would have to worry about. But at the same time it made her feel bad, because she wasn't in love with David.

Daddy would be shocked to know what David was counting on when he could drive and they could single-date two nights a weekend. She knew that her mom knew, because they had talked about things like how far you should go and how you didn't want to be cheap. Her mom had talked to her about how hard it was to draw the line back once you had let him do something. And she had promised that she would never do that, not at her age, not in high school, really let him do it or anything.

She knew her daddy and her mom trusted her.

But she didn't feel that she would be letting them down if she showed David once, because she and he had been going together a long time, and they had got to the place where he expected that. Leslie had done more than that with Jimmy, but she was in love with Jimmy. Leslie had never wanted to go with anyone else, and she talked about him all the time. She wanted to get married someday, and said she felt they were secretly engaged, is why she let Jimmy do the things she did.

Jeanetta took her clothes off, to see what she looked like in the mirrored walls. Her breasts weren't huge, but they were a lot bigger than they looked in her clothes. You could get the idea in her pink sweater, but you couldn't really see the way you could in the mirrors.

She turned the dimmer switch and let herself look at herself in the low light in all directions. She imagined herself in front of mirrors in the dressing rooms when she went shopping or at school in the bathroom, and tried to figure if those showed the same Jeanetta that these did.

She wouldn't have minded taking all her clothes off, like now, for her biology teacher, Mr. Jenkins. Even though he was older, he was a lot more her type of person than David. Besides, he had been married, so he was used to seeing a woman naked, and it wouldn't bother him. His marriage hadn't worked out, because she had probably been an uncaring person or fat or something. But he would have done it with his wife, for a number of years, so he would be used to seeing you.

Mr. Jenkins was a runner. He had an athlete's body. That was unusual in someone like a biology teacher, that you usually thought of as a studious type. The only way you could know that he wasn't an athlete was he wore glasses.

One reason Jeanetta had helped get the Jay-Teens signed up to go to the School for the Deaf was because she could tell Mr. Jenkins about it, as, being in biology, he would know about congenital hearing loss. She knew he could have been a great doctor, except that he got married when it was a mistake and had to go to work right away and teach.

. . . Jeanetta made herself go back and tell the truth. She tried to be an honest person all the time, even to herself, even when she was imagining. The truth was that Mr. Jenkins was still married, and his wife was very pretty and not old or fat. Jeanetta had seen her at Parents' Night, because she had come to help out.

Her feelings for Mr. Jenkins were a secret, because not only her mom didn't know about it, but Leslie didn't. That was because Leslie was in love with Jimmy and would be shocked.

Jeanetta felt like crying thinking about it, having a secret from even her best friend, who she told everything, but that must be part of getting to be fifteen and growing up.

She was ashamed of herself for her thoughts and for feeling weepy on her birthday, almost her birthday, when that should be the happiest day of the year.

She went in to take a bath and get dressed for tonight. She had a private bath now, because when she started junior high Daddy and her mom had given her their bedroom with the bath opening off of it, and they had taken the smaller bedroom that used the bath in the hall, which was also for company. She was of an age to need the privacy, her mom had said. Daddy had pretended to make a fuss about it, but she knew that he didn't mind. And it did give you a feeling of being grown, to have a bath all to yourself, because you could walk in there to get cleaned up without having to put your clothes back on. And when Leslie spent the night, they didn't have to go out in the hall in their pajamas in the middle of the night.

She decided to wear the new outfit she had, that David would like, because he always liked her to dress up. It was a cashmere sweater and solid skirt with pleats on one side. She wanted to look extra nice for him tonight so that he wouldn't be disappointed in her.

But first, when Daddy came home, she would spend some time with him and her mom, the way she had told them she would. Because she knew Daddy had something for her, and that he wanted her there by herself for a while before David came, so he could give it to her.

She loved Daddy and her mom a lot because they liked to make a special occasion out of everything. She always had packages with ribbons on them—sometimes one or two would be tucked away somewhere like the linen closet or pantry so she would get to hunt for it—and a big pink Valentine cake with flowers made out of icing.

She had guessed already what the surprise was for this year: they meant to let her open a checking account, now that she was old enough. But she would pretend to be surprised. She bet they would have pink checks with her name on them already printed up: *Jeanetta Edna Mayfield*.

Betty and Finis

———————◆———————

B E T T Y wished she really was Jeanetta's mother. She was somewhat older than the average to be the mother of a fifteen-year-old, as she and Finis had waited five years before they admitted that they weren't going to have a baby.

She hadn't made him go through those awful tests where they find out whose fault it is if you don't get pregnant; that didn't matter anyway, whose fault. Besides, she knew that it was hers. Her own mother had been such a busy person, always trying to get her name or picture in the paper, that she had never had time to talk to Betty about things; and even though it didn't make sense if you looked straight at it, Betty was convinced that you didn't learn how to have a baby unless your mother was the kind that talked to you about it. Which is why she talked to Jeanetta about all the facts and what they meant in your life.

Her own mother, Betty's, had been so busy that she wouldn't let Betty and her brother stack the dinner plates; that way the bottoms didn't get dirty and they didn't have to wash anything but the tops. That's how busy she was. She was gone from home more than a working mother, trying to better herself with clubwork, get her name in some program or herself on some committee.

Because they weren't exactly mother and daughter, Betty had always felt that she and Jeanetta were more like sisters. She would hold her and feed her and it was just the way her friends had done with their little sisters. She had always wanted to have a bunch of little sisters; she didn't like being the only girl at home. Her oldest brother hadn't been close to her at all. In fact, he still wasn't, and hardly ever came around. He didn't like Finis, whom he called a go-getter, and he always said it in a derogatory way. As if he was superior to Finis, which he wasn't. But Finis said brokers were like that: their money went to their head, which was the wrong location from where it belonged. He didn't like her brother either; it was mutual. He said he put on too many airs for a four-eyed, left-footed jerk named Jack.

Sometimes it made her feel that she was in the middle of two kids, two brothers almost. And then her relationship with Jeanetta was the calming influence. That's when it was like having a sister. Jeanetta was the only real girlfriend that Betty had ever had.

It was no wonder she hadn't been able to sleep all night long for worrying about today.

She remembered how nervous and excited she had been when they picked the baby's name. It had been the biggest, most important decision they made—after deciding to let Mack, the minister, find them a baby through a doctor friend and not through an agency in Louisville.

"It's the law of averages we'll get a better kid," Finis had said about going through Mack. "Somebody of good cloth who's in trouble is more likely to turn up than somebody who has to move to a home and wait it out. You don't know the first thing about those kids. Not the number-one first thing. Mack and his old buddy the doctor, they know the inside story. They wouldn't pull one over on Finis Mayfield because they know I'd be on their backs in a week if they tried. You're always going to have your person in trouble. 'Man that is born of woman is of few days and full of trouble.' "

Whenever he said something like that, Betty knew that he was quoting from the Masonic funeral service. He was a Mason and proud of it and had memorized the service for when his time came to be the one to say it. The service was a secret, but she could tell when he would give a line from it, as it wasn't in his natural way of speaking.

Sometimes when he would leave for work, when he was in a good mood, he'd hold her up close and say: " 'Twilight and evening bells and after that the dark; and may there be no sadness of farewell when I embark.' " He had a rolling way he said the words that made you happy. He would recite something sometimes if he had coaxed her out of her gown and got her relaxed enough until she wanted him to make love to her. (Which was hard at the beginning: when she realized that she couldn't have babies, she had frozen up when he touched her. But he had persevered and stayed gentle and she had learned to come around to him.) Those times he would say something that he had changed around from the ceremony: " 'Soft and safe to you, my Betty, be this mortal bed, bright and beautiful be thy rising from it.' " And she would almost want to cry. That was as close as he could come, sing-songing it that way as if it was a joke, to saying how he felt.

The name for the baby had almost caused them a fight.

He had wanted her named after his mother, Edna, but Betty couldn't imagine a girl going through school called Edna and having a single solitary friend or date. Could you picture a cheerleader named Edna? But she hadn't wanted to hurt the feelings of her mother-in-law, whom she didn't like to begin with (she was very possessive). "We could make Edna the middle name." Betty tried that idea as a compromise. She suggested to Finis that the baby would get off to a better start with a name of her very own that wasn't already someone's name. That could put you in a shadow position, it seemed to her.

The night Mack called that the baby had come and it was a girl, they got the hat out.

They'd worked this all out before so they wouldn't end up having hard feelings. They each put their four favorite names on slips of paper and put them in a hat. But they agreed they wouldn't draw until the baby was there, and for sure all right and going to be theirs. That was so they wouldn't have a name picked out and then lose the baby.

Betty had always hated her first name. It was very common, for one thing. Most Bettys at least were short for Elizabeth, but she wasn't. She had desperately wanted to change it to Beth or Betsy when she was in high school, but her mother had thrown a hissy fit. So she had stuck with Betty. But she wanted something special for her daughter.

The names she wrote out and put in were: Kimberly, Deborah, Susannah, and Jeanetta. Jeanetta, her favorite, was for Jeanette MacDonald, whom her daddy considered the best singer in the world. She had changed it a little, by adding the *a* on the end, to make it three syllables. She had read that if your last name had two syllables, then you wanted a first name with either one or three, for contrast. Since one-syllable names didn't sound enough to Betty— Jane, Gail, names like that—she had made all of hers three.

Finis had gone in for fancy names: Nicole, Michelle, Nadine, Babette. He didn't go along with her three-syllable theory because he said if you had a long name like that, then it got shortened into a nickname, and his names were not something that anybody would end up with a nick-name for.

They almost got into a fight about that. He would say that she was going to have a Kim or Debbie or Sue or Jean, so what was the point in the long name? And she would fly off at him and say that he was picking those high-sounding French names to make her mad because he wanted to name their baby Edna and he wasn't really trying to come up with anything else. She hated the sing-song sound of all his names: Michelle Mayfield, Nicole Mayfield. She could hardly even think about them.

She liked the name Mayfield; it was very beautiful for a name. She had liked Betty a lot better when she became Betty Mayfield than she had before, and sometimes she could actually forget that she had lived twenty years of her life as Betty Sharp. Betty Sharp was about as bad a name as you could get. It had sounded like Beauty Shop to her ever since some boy in the second grade had called her that. When she got married she had thought a lot about changing it all the way: to Beth Mayfield. But by that time Finis had already got his special nickname for her, Betty Boop, and he wouldn't hear of it.

So, once they knew for sure the baby was theirs, they had the drawing. Betty was almost sick with thinking that it would be one of Finis's names, but not wanting, when they were so happy, to let herself mind too much. Finis had insisted that he would do the drawing. Which she didn't like, either, but she didn't say so. As it turned out, her fingers were so sticky that she wouldn't have been able to pull anything out of the hat anyway. They were clammy with sweat.

"Now, we're agreed to this?" Finis had asked.

"Yes." She nodded. "Whatever you draw is it. We won't change our minds." She felt herself shaking all over.

With a flourish he had dashed his hand in faster than you could watch and pulled out a slip of folded paper which he handed her to read: JEANETTA.

She was almost sick to her stomach in relief. Her hand had almost dropped it ten times trying to unfold it. She hugged him and couldn't make any sound come out she was so glad.

"That suit you?" he asked.

"Yes, oh, yes." She had felt lightheaded as a roller-coaster ride. "Do you mind?"

"See for yourself if it's all right with me." He had handed her the hat. "Take a look," he pressed her. "Take a look at all the names."

One at a time she opened the seven slips of paper left: JEANETTA   JEANETTA   JEANETTA   JEANETTA   JEANETTA JEANETTA   JEANETTA.

She had absolutely bawled then. She'd been so keyed up she hadn't noticed that the slip of paper she'd read first was in his handwriting.

"Oh, Finis—" She buried her face in his shoulder. "What a trick you played on me."

"I didn't care that much, Boop. It seemed to me that you did. 'We are reminded of the purity of life and recti-tude of conduct.' I thought my Betty deserved it." He swung her around. "What I did was decide which of yours I liked the best, and let that do."

It was a happy day.

Finis was too good to her, she knew it herself. For fifteen years, every time it was Jeanetta's birthday, he had tried to goad her into telling their daughter the truth. But every year she had wanted to wait, just one more year. A little girl was fragile, and you didn't want to do something that would break the closeness you had with her.

She thought if Jeanetta found out that her natural mother had been a girl *like that*, instead of the mother she trusted and thought was hers, and was hers as far as raising was concerned, that she might go wild. You read about things like that. Get pregnant herself. When she'd talked to Mack about waiting just a little longer, though, maybe until Jeanetta was sixteen, he had sided with Finis: "If you don't tell her now, Betty Girl, you're going to be in a heap of trouble for sure."

The men had in mind the fact that a lot of things came into your life in high school that required birth certificates, such as your driver's education and your Social Security, should you get a part-time job—all kinds of things. Later the girls and boys would be making a trip abroad maybe, on a tour, when they were seniors. You couldn't tell. They had started her at Miss Feenie's school, so there hadn't been any trouble about having to show anything to the school, but now the men insisted that there was going to be trouble. Jeanetta would be sure to find out one way or the other. "It's the Law of Averages" was how Finis put it.

He was a Life Underwriter and that was his way of talking. Betty knew that was just his manner; that he loved their daughter as much as she did.

"Do we have to?" she asked now, knowing that it was settled and there was no backing out. "I don't see why we have to."

"Now, Boop, we agreed."

"I feel it will break something. Like the Haviland platter of Mother's that got cracked the day after Dad died. They had carried it with them all those years, in every move, their prize wedding present, and the maid just happened to crack it that very same day. I'm not naturally superstitious, but I feel it will never be the same."

"We waited too long as it is, that was your doing. Not being able to bring yourself to tell her. It would have been a lot better if she'd known from the start."

"I wanted her to feel secure."

"A fifteen-year-old couldn't be more secure unless she owned a bank. Everything she wants, we give it. Our bedroom, you'll recall."

"She needed her privacy."

"The head of the household has to move his belongings from the master bedroom to the guest quarters so his daughter can grow up in style?"

"She needed the private bath. When Leslie spends the night, they can't be walking down the hall in their pajamas, or when David's waiting and she's getting fixed up."

"I have to shave in public view of the Fuller Brush Man?"

"Oh, Finis, be serious. When did we ever have a Fuller Brush Man come to call on us since we were children?"

"The Avon Lady?"

Finis was a good life-insurance salesman, because he believed in his job: that you should take care of your loved ones. But he did it with a light touch. He was much in demand for after-dinner talks. He was a member of the Toastmasters' Club of Paducah. Betty was proud of him.

But he looked at this from a man's perspective, a business-man's. When you were about to break something precious, you didn't make jokes about Avon Calling.

Betty didn't want how it was with Jeanetta to change, not the slightest bit. They were closer than most mothers and daughters; Jeanetta confided in her nearly everything. And what she couldn't say, Betty guessed. She knew that Jeanetta wasn't in love with David, a thing which Finis couldn't see before his eyes—that's because he liked the boy and his family. But a mother naturally sensed those things. Which is why she wanted Jeanetta to be careful with herself.

She had talked with Mack about her fear that Jeanetta would get pregnant and have to drop out of school. She thought maybe it was because, deep down, she was afraid that Jeanetta would turn out like her natural mother. But Mack said that was because she, Betty, had never got preg-nant, so she thought it was something easy that just hap-pened to girls. That Jeanetta was not about to do a dumb thing like that, any more than Betty would have when she was that age, if she could have.

Mack hadn't told them the name of the doctor or the real parents, although the doctor was dead now, he did tell that, which was a relief, because then you weren't tempted to try to find things out. He had told them that he trusted the doctor like his own daddy, and that it was a doctor's baby, and that the mother was a good girl.

She didn't think Finis ever gave a thought to the natural mother. He had the personality that could accept things. He had given up the idea of a son without so much as a backward glance when they decided she couldn't have chil-dren. "A girl's fine," he said. And he had got to thinking from the first day of the pretty little baby as their own.

"Possession is nine-tenths of the law," he'd say that first month, calming Betty down. "Pretty as a picture. Looks just like me."

"If we could wait till Sunday?" She knew this was clinging to a last hope, the relief of a two-day delay. "Let her have dinner out with David, and her cake and presents the same as always tomorrow, and spend the night with Leslie. Maybe after church?"

"David isn't going to care where those knockers came from originally, honey."

"Finis!" She blushed a deep blush. Because she sometimes thought about that, too, but it wasn't something you wanted to say out loud.

"At ease, Boop, I'm not casting aspersions on the character of our exemplary daughter, or on David Foster personally, a boy, as you know, I like a lot, as well as his father and mother, but rather making an observation about human nature. That's my business: to know the laws of human nature. 'Here we behold the narrow house appointed for all living.'" He came and sat beside his wife on the peach brocade sofa he had given her last year when she'd redecorated the living room so Jeanetta could have David over on double dates with Pam and Jeff. "I'm trying to calm you down, now. No backing out. We agreed."

As long as she could think she was Jeanetta's mother and that they were closer than any mother and daughter she knew, then Betty didn't have to look straight at any of the things she might not be doing right. Part of her fear was that if Jeanetta knew the truth, she'd begin to think that maybe this person named Betty was not as good a mother as there could be, and she'd not be as satisfied or want to share things with her anymore. Jeanetta might wish, as long as it wasn't a matter of nature, that she'd got a completely different type of mother altogether. The way Betty herself had, growing up.

"Would you want Mack to come do it for us? That Christian has a heart as big as the Kiwanis Club budget and a head just as full of padding. He might tell her that the fairies brought her; I'm not sure he's ever got himself a firm grasp on the facts of life. The day he should have got himself instructed on the purpose of his calling, to 'look down with infinite compassion upon the widow and fatherless in the hour of their desolation,' he was absent with an attack of the chest cold. He thinks God is the Big Fund Raiser in the Sky. But—" he put his arm around her—"if you'd sit easier, Boop, with the man of the cloth handing out the news, I'll go along."

She knew Finis was not blaspheming, because he said these very things to Mack to his face when they had the minister to dinner. Mack didn't take offense. They were friends. Mack said, "You play the Law of Averages in your job, Mr. Fine-Ass, and I play the Law of Avarice in mine. If the I.R.S. didn't squeeze, none of that green would ever land in the lap of the Lord, I'll tell you that. I make it easy, is all."

Finis always said after one of those conversations that he thought the Methodist Church was more like his lodge, and the Masons were more like his church. And that he must be one turned-around Life Underwriter.

Betty knew it would hurt him a lot to let Mack tell something that personal and important to Jeanetta. So she shook her head no. "It needs to be us. I just wish we didn't have to do it."

"You should have thought of that fact fifteen years ago when we were preparing to put the names in the hat for Miss Jeanetta Edna Mayfield. Mack and me and the half-blind old doc should have extracted a promise from Betty Sharp Mayfield herself: Do you, Betty Boop, beloved wife of Finis Mayfield, C.L.U., solemnly swear not to deceive the upcoming bundle of God's love past half-a-score-and-five years . . ."

"Oh, honey, I'm scared."

When Jeanetta came into the peach-and-green living room, her parents were hugging on the sofa. But Betty was not embarrassed. It was good for a girl to see that her mom and daddy loved each other. Betty did not have a single recollection of ever seeing her own mother and father hug. Her mom was too busy getting her name in the paper, and her daddy had business worries. They didn't have the same values that she and Finis did. He had changed more than her name for the better when he married her.

Their daughter bent down and kissed both their cheeks. "Does this look okay, Mom?" She modeled her new cashmere sweater and pleated skirt. The sweater was soft as feathers. Their daughter did look beautiful. Her features were regular, with a kind of small nose and eyes that slanted up just a little at the corners. Her best feature, though, was her hair, which was long and shiny blonde, and came past her shoulders in the back and was feathered away from her cheeks on each side. Betty felt so proud. She had made such a pretty girl. She knew it was your mother who contributed to that. Nobody but your mother took care of you every day and looked after you and taught you what to wear with what and how to fix up but not so much that it showed. Nobody else did that.

The only way it seemed she didn't take after them was in how short she was. But that was pleasing in a girl.

"I better send a po-lice escort out with you and David."

Finis made a mock scowl, pretending to be scared to let her go out.

"Daddy!" Jeanetta pretended to be shocked.

That was something they always did, before every date. Betty was envious. She had not had that, growing up, and it would have made you feel that you were really valuable to your daddy. That was something nobody but a daddy could do for you. Maybe until you got married.

Of course, a daddy didn't know all the things about you that your mother did; a mother and daughter shared secrets, but that was in the nature of things.

"You look fine," Betty told her daughter. "Maybe just a little more eye shadow, at the corners?"

"I had more on and wiped it off. I wasn't sure."

"I think you could add a little."

Jeanetta's daddy didn't feel as calm as he presented himself. His deportment and his demeanor belied the depth of his concern. He held himself responsible for the trust they were about to break on this winter evening: he had let himself be persuaded by his wife to go along with this delay against his better judgment. Only a few times in his life had Finis Mayfield ever let that happen, at least in his business. But home was a different matter. In such an environment your feelings took on a different persuasion.

He wanted nothing more in this sinful, wayward world than to make his Jeanetta happy. She had turned out to be more joy than he'd thought a man entitled to. She had the good spirit of his mother, herself a persistent true Christian (not in the same league as their current pastor, by a long shot). But not by any stretch was this same mother, a steadfast woman, what you could call lovely to look at. He never blamed her for that, as she had come from a lifetime of scrimping and saving; still, it delighted him that his Jeanetta had the outright attractiveness of his wife. That was the joy. His girl was pretty as a picture, which he took pleasure in afresh each time she came into his line of sight, the more so as he remained convinced that, had it been his doing, he could never have created anything half as pleasureful to gaze upon. It followed then that he wanted mightily for her to know, now that they were about to tell her the truth, that he considered the way she had come to them the best thing that could have happened to a father such as himself.

With this on his mind, Finis patted the space beside him. "Sit down, JeanEddie, squeeze right in here by your daddy." That was his nickname for her, combining both names. He thought that for your special ones you should come up with something in the nature of a private language.

Daintily she sat between them on the sofa and waited.

" 'Nor will the innocence of youth or the charm of beauty propitiate our purpose.' Which translates as: we've got something on our minds, honey."

"Okay, Daddy," she said, smiling her trust at him.

He put his arm around her, and his wife reached out and took their daughter's hand in hers. There was no getting around one fact: there were two scared parents in that redecorated living room. "Your mom won't settle down if I don't get to the matter at hand—"

"What, Daddy?" His little girl looked excited, like she was pretending to go along with him about a surprise, but safe in her knowledge that nothing was really going to happen. She looked the way she did when she waited for a birthday present which she knew was forthcoming. Part of the procedure was to let her daddy tease her for a spell before presenting it.

"Oakey doakey, JeanEddie, here goes." He made himself get calm. "Once upon a time, in the sight of God, 'to whom the secrets of all hearts are as an open book,' there was a beautiful young bride whose heart had closed in grief."

Jeanette looked puzzled, but she still smiled at him and listened dutifully.

". . . So some kind doctor comes along and sees her misery, and persuades her to unburden herself. 'What is it, lovely lady?' he asks, and she tells him, 'It is my fondest wish to have a little baby girl.' 'Then you shall have one, my dear,' he says, and he goes out and finds a baby who needs a home full of welcome and dispensing love, and, in due time, no less than a private bath and a daddy willing to shave in full sight of the Avon Lady . . ."

He could feel a change in their daughter. The shoulder beneath his arm was still; it seemed to have shrunk.

"What, Daddy?" She asked him again, but now she turned and looked at her mother's face, her eyes not understanding. "What, Mom?"

"In time," he continued steadily, "Betty and Finis Mayfield were blessed with the one perfect chosen daughter, and they named her Jeanetta Edna, because they loved her most."

He stopped. He sought to maintain his method of mixing the serious and the light.

Their daughter turned from one to the other. "Daddy? Mom? What does he mean?"

"We picked you out, honey," Betty answered, her voice conveying her definite uncertainty.

25

"Picked me out?" Jeanetta looked at them. She looked the way she had as a little girl when something had gone wrong or got mixed up in the grown-ups' language.

He told her about fixing up the little bedroom for her, about the pink quilted bassinet and the Teddy Bear mobiles. He went over the first days that she already had snapshots of. It wasn't anything new—their anticipation and delight in her arrival. But he said it all again to her.

"There was no contest, JeanEddie. You were the fairest of them all."

In the crowded space on the sofa, his own and only daughter finally asked: "Am I adopted?"

" 'To take voluntarily into a relationship,' the good book Dictionary says. That's it." Finis had read that definition beforehand to Betty. He'd rejected the one that said: "to take up from another and use as one's own," though he knew that it was partly true. It was for yourself that you did it.

"But you never told me." Jeanetta's voice sounded hurt and far away.

"We never needed to before. But now you're getting to be a grown-up girl."

"How old was I?"

"Just born."

"Who were . . . they?"

"The father—" Finis could not say *your* father—"was a doctor. We don't know about the mother, but she had the proper credentials. We don't know who gave you to us, honey, but if we did we'd thank them every day."

In a small voice Jeanetta asked, "Does David know?"

Betty answered quickly. "No, that's up to you. We wouldn't have told somebody like that first." But her voice still had a quaver to it which showed her unease.

"Mack knows," he added his own bit, "our worldly minister of God's grace. He, in fact, was responsible for our finding such a perfect baby daughter."

"Reverend Jones knows?" Jeanetta turned her face away. "Grandma?"

Betty tried to soothe her. "Our families had to know, since I wasn't pregnant."

"Uncle Jack that you hate, Daddy?"

"Our kin needed to know, JeanEd. It was good news that we wanted to share."

She scooted out from between them on the sofa and got up. She wouldn't look them in the face, but wrapped her arms around herself and studied the floor. "But I'm not a kinfolk, am I, so I didn't have to know?"

"Now, baby—"

"That's what you're really telling me, isn't it? That I'm not even as much kin as Uncle Jack that you hate." She ran to the door, her face looking shut to them.

He had no answer.

"Can I tell?" she asked. "David and Leslie?"

"Sure, honey." He stood and held his arms out to her. "Tell whosomever you want." But she had got a long way out of his reach. "You're a big girl now."

And she was, too, at that minute. Framed in the doorway, his little girl was grown and gone away.

"Okay, Daddy," she said in a high voice. "Or should I call you *Mr. Mayfield?*" They could hear her crying as she slammed her door.

They sat beside each other and let it grow dark without moving to turn on a lamp. Finally Finis put his arm around his wife. " 'Let us therefore embrace the present moment, while time and opportunity are at our disposal, to provide

27

against that great change which we know, full well, must come. . . .' "

Betty could feel his hurt alongside hers, but she didn't let on. She knew she had done wrong making them wait, but she couldn't see it any other way. She had only wanted to do what Finis did when they drew names: repeat a thing over and over until it came true.

Jeanetta on Jeanetta

S H E waked Monday morning with a sudden flush of shame, the way you do if you've done something awful and forgotten it while you were asleep, and then, as you begin to wake, it hits you again that you did it, and you want to die.

That had happened to her before. Once when she had run for cheerleader, in junior high, and they had been sure the three of them would get it, Leslie and her and Pam, and Leslie had and Pam had, but she hadn't. They had always talked about how they would do it together, and for months they had practiced for the tryouts. Then she'd lost to someone they hardly knew; and somebody told somebody else that Jeanetta was too stiff to be a cheerleader. Jeanetta couldn't get over that, the idea that all the time she had thought she was a *limber* person—all the time she and Leslie had talked about getting limber, or staying limber—she had been *stiff* and didn't know about it. At no time when she looked at herself in the bathroom mirror had she seen that she was stiff. She had wanted to crawl in a hole and never come out.

When her mom heard about the new cheerleaders, she

said: "I thought you were going to try out, honey," and Jeanetta told her that she'd got over wanting to do that months ago.

That wasn't the only time that shame had made her tell Daddy and her mom a lie. The other time was the piano recital. Her face still got hot, recalling that. She had taken music for six years, and Daddy and her mom had got her a fruitwood console-type piano that matched the furniture in the living room, and they went around being proud that she could play it.

But what they didn't realize was that she never practiced at home. She did that at school in the music room or at her teacher's house when no one was taking lessons. So Daddy and her mom had only heard her at recitals, and at all the ones before the last she had remembered what the teacher said: "Don't be strident, Jeanetta, don't bang."

But the year she quit she had been the last number on the program, and she had a good piece, a big piece, and when she got up to play she got into the music and that's all that was on her mind; when she finished she would probably have started all over and played it again from the beginning, louder, if everyone hadn't clapped.

Her mom had been embarrassed, although she made excuses for Jeanetta, the way she always did: "Honey," she said, "why in the world didn't Miss Crispin give you a recital number which matched the other girls'?"

She never took another lesson. She wouldn't talk to the teacher when she called. She told her mom that they had done hearing tests at school and that she'd found out she was tone deaf, so that was what was the matter. Her mom didn't mind: the piano looked nice in the living room, and when they'd redecorated last year, with the peach sofa and green carpet, they'd had a portrait painted of Jeanetta, aged five, in a peach dress. To hang over the fruitwood piano.

She had felt bad about herself those times: that she was not limber enough to be a cheerleader, which she knew her mom wanted; that she stood out from the rest by banging at her recital. But this was different. Those had been her fault. This time it was them, it was Daddy and her mom who had done the lying. And they didn't even know that everything had changed. They didn't even care.

Friday night, after they told her, she'd fixed her face with a little extra eye shadow, brushed her hair again, and gone right out with David when he came. She didn't want him to know that anything was wrong, since he had counted on tonight, and was taking her to a steak place that had really high prices.

After they ate—steak and rolls, and she had corn on the cob, and he had a baked potato with everything and a large Coke—he explained about the change of plans. They were supposed to go to the movie and then wait for his father at the ice-cream place, but David made her say that she would go to his house instead. He knew his house would be empty, as his parents were at supper with some people that they saw every Friday night. (His parents had more of a crowd than hers did; they were more social types, but in a friendly, not a climbing, way.) She told him she would, but at the same time she felt ashamed of their taking advantage of his mother and father, who liked her a lot, or all the time told David that they did. It didn't seem honest.

Their going to his house made her nervous, and she

31

guessed David knew that, because on the way he kept squeezing her hand, and finally he asked right out: "You going to?"

"Not right here, silly." She made out like she didn't understand, but that was her way of letting him know she meant yes (any time you didn't tell a boy no, that was a way of saying yes) and he understood and got real excited and put his arm around her waist.

His family's living room was big and kind of a gameroom compared to hers, with a pool table at one end and a bunch of dart boards and things like that. As soon as they got there David opened a Coke and then, right away, he turned down the lamp and began to kiss her and pester her about taking off her sweater so he could look. "You promised." He was telling her he loved her and that he was going crazy and that when was she going to do it, and that she'd promised.

"I have to tell you something first, David."

"Jesus, what, can't it wait?"

"It's already waited."

"You're having your period? That's okay. Jesus. I'm just going to look."

"Not that." She felt herself blush. "Something else."

"Okay." He quit pestering, but he had his arms around her and was moving one hand around on her back.

In a whisper she told him that her mom and daddy were not really her daddy and mom, that she was adopted, which meant that she was *illegitimate*. She told him about how she was first mad, and then hurt, and then ashamed, and how she couldn't get it off her mind.

He acted at first like it was funny and didn't mean anything. "Hurry up and get your sweater off, then, before we find out we're brother and sister." He could be half-serious and half-funny like her daddy when he wanted to. He made out like he was grabbing her in a big hurry and kissed at her ear. "That's what always happens in the movies."

So she tried to laugh and get it off her mind. She let him kiss her the way he liked to, for a long time, and then, without him having to ask again, she began to pull off her cashmere sweater, and then she unhooked the bra in the front, because he couldn't get the hang of it, and then she sat there in the dim light, showing him her breasts, and it was something that felt satisfying, like she needed to do it as much as he wanted her to.

He pretended to go wild when he saw them and made a noise like Tarzan and ran around the room and beat his chest, and then came back and held her and began to feel her breasts and his face got a really funny look. She hadn't known that he would touch her. She'd thought he would look, the way she did at herself, to see what they were like. But he wanted to touch them and kiss her at the same time, and when he did that she felt a lot like crying, and she didn't want him to do it anymore, and she put her things back on.

"We've got another hour, over an hour," he said. "Come on. Jeannie, come on. You hardly let me do anything." He was squirming around and his face was red and he kept trying to get her sweater off again.

"I took it off." She put her head on his shoulder. "Don't pester me any more." He was still straightening his clothes and making a lot of breathing noise, the way he did in the back seat, and she waited until he had calmed down. "How do you really feel about it, David?"

"They're great. They're the most beautiful tits I ever saw, they're the only live ones. I mean it. Come on, Jeannie."

She nestled her head on his shoulder. "Not that." Her voice was muffled against his shirt. "What I told you."

"Don't turn out to be my sister, will you?" He kept trying to lift her head for another kiss.

"Really."

He let her go and gave up. "My Uncle Bud almost adopted."

"I thought they had four kids."

"Yeah. He makes the joke that it took him six years to get the combination and six more to turn it off."

"But he and your aunt were going to?" Jeanetta felt better. She'd met his aunt and uncle, and they were nice people.

"Yeah, they talked about it. But then they decided not to."

"Why?"

"Because Uncle Bud says you don't know what you're getting into. They had friends who adopted who had nothing but trouble. He dropped out of school, the kid, and went kind of crazy. It was in his blood or something. So they decided not to. Like if they hadn't had my oldest cousin right then they'd probably have gone into the import-export business or something. Something where they traveled, which they're always talking about that they wanted to do. I feel sorry for my cousins: how would you like to grow up knowing you'd kept your folks from being in the import-export business—?"

Then Jeanetta sat up and she was still. She wished she hadn't kept her promise, or even gone out with him at all. Sometimes you find out about somebody you've known forever and gone steady with a year that you didn't know him at all.

"Let's go home," she said.

"I *am* home." He couldn't figure it out, and kept trying to be funny and put his arms around her, but all he did was make it worse.

"Let's go wait for your daddy."

"One more time," he begged. "Just one more time. We can't sit eating ice cream all night. One more time, Jeannie, come on. I won't get my license for three more months. I could die in that time. Please." He tried to kiss her and pull at her sweater at the same time.

"I don't want to any more."

"Did I make you mad or something? Me and my big mouth. Did I? Your folks didn't want to be world travelers, for Christ's sake, or they would have. They wanted you, which is more than my cousins can say, is all I meant. For Christ's sake. Come on."

But she had gone away. In her mind they had broken up and she didn't feel anything for him at all any more.

After a little while he got the idea, and they went to the ice-cream parlor where they were supposed to wait after the movie. He got Rocky Road, which he always did, and she got Jamoca Almond, which she didn't finish. David told her what Jeff had told him the movie was about. She didn't care, and her folks weren't going to ask her the whole plot, and anyway she wasn't going to tell *Mrs. Mayfield* about her date. But she let David talk so they would have something to do until his father drove up.

When they dropped her off she ran into the house before David could walk her to the door. Inside, she headed for her room.

"Did you have a good time, honey?" Her mom looked anxious.

"It was okay."

"Want something to eat?" Her mom was in her robe, waiting, with hot chocolate and marshmallows fixed on the kitchen table.

"No thanks."

"Sit a minute and tell me about the movie."

"I'm really tired, okay?" She went in her room and closed the door after her; and, for the first time in her life, tucked herself in bed.

She had wanted to call Leslie when she got in from her date, but she didn't. She thought maybe David had told Jimmy that they'd had a fight, and Leslie would want to know all about what happened. But when she got to Leslie's Saturday, that was brushed aside. "You didn't break up with David, silly, just because he was a dummy. What was he supposed to do, faint?" What proved that she and Leslie were best friends was that Leslie wanted to talk right away about Jeanetta's real news. "Why didn't you tell me the very exact minute you knew? It's so fantastic. It's so dramatic."

"How could I? You don't have a phone in the back seat of Jimmy's car," Jeanetta teased her.

"I'm sick green with envy, I mean it."

Jeanetta could relax a little and get used to the idea through hearing Leslie talk about it. She felt safe at Leslie's house, because they could be private here, as Leslie's mom slept downstairs and there was nobody to hear them.

Leslie was sitting cross-legged and bouncing up and down. "You're lucky, you know that? Remember all those times I used to tell you how I went around making up these parents who were not really mine, not the pair I got stuck with who are the worst you can imagine, and you would argue that yours were the kindest and sweetest of all the parents in the world. Well, you're lucky, is all I can say."

"You're just saying that."

"I am, because it's the truth. Here is my mother running a radio plant-talk show. I could die. Fourteen kids a week wait for me in the hall and quote her to me: 'When a plant has a temper tantrum, dears, you water the phooey out of it.' She says that every week, I swear. 'Don't water the phooey out of it.' 'If your yellow leaves are experiencing shock, dears, you just rummage your finger around until it's cool and wet.' 'Where you been rummaging your finger lately, Les?' I could die. She tells the old ladies out there, 'Wait till it's retreated down two inches.' I wish I was an orphan."

Jeanetta knew that Leslie secretly enjoyed her mother being on the radio and sort of famous, and being teased about it. She knew that Leslie didn't mean what she was saying, that it was her way of trying to get Jeanetta used to the new idea of who she was.

Leslie always talked like she hated her mother, but Jeanetta didn't ever believe her. Mrs. Richards was nice and would always say to Jeanetta, "Move in, honey, you're a good influence." Though she did seem more casual and what you would think of an adopted mother as being than her own mom.

"I remind you that my grandmother packed her bags in the middle of my mom's wedding reception, caught a plane, and left her husband and the whole works. Her job was done that minute and she wasn't even staying for a cup of

37

punch. It's no wonder my mom half the time forgets my name. I mean, you know your folks wanted you. You're lucky."

"What do you *really* think?" They were sitting on the bed in their cotton pajamas. They had just washed their hair and were talking above the sound of the blow dryers. It was a way to say a lot without looking right at each other. At their age, you didn't want to get too close even when you were talking about private things. When they finished their hair they'd put on their coats and take a walk around the block, rolling up their pajamas, or putting their jeans on top, but knowing they were outside walking in pajamas. It would be really cold, so they would huddle over, and that was a good time to talk, too. In the dark.

When they were little they would roll each other's hair and eat huge bowls of ice cream, but now they didn't do that, because they were trying to stay thin, and because they were more self-conscious now than then.

"What I think—" Leslie spoke slowly, the way she did when she was studying—"is that you'd be really mad at them."

"Who?"

"The Mr. and Mrs. Mayfield."

"Oh, I thought you meant the real ones."

"No, dummy, you can't get mad at *them*. Think about your mother. Fifteen years ago if you got pregnant, what could you do? Kill yourself or put it up. He was probably married, so what could she do? You're a love child."

"Oh." Jeanetta said the words over to herself, wondering if she looked like a love child.

"Sure. A love child. But I'd think you'd be red-hot mad at the Mr. and Mrs. Mayfield, that they could just up and take you, without giving anybody else a shot at you. Not that you got the worst parents in the world, like I have, not by any means, but that you didn't have a say. You were at the mercy of whatever busybody couple came along and decided that they deserved a baby that day and they'd take you. With your real parents you just have to lump it, but with the other kind you can always think that if they hadn't nosy-parkered in and grabbed, you might have been the answer to a prayer for some beautiful rich couple who was dying of love and lived on the Riviera and wanted to coddle you and spoil you and raise you to be a famous foundling. But anyway, at least you can be a love child, so that's something."

A foundling. Jeanetta turned the hot air of the blower against her cheek. Leslie was more adventurous than she was. If it had happened to Leslie, she would have made a big story out of it, told everyone at Tilghman High, and everyone would have envied her. Jeanetta couldn't do that. She felt her face turn red with embarrassment, but left the blower on it, letting that be the cause.

"I guess you better be grateful it was who it was, though. Look at it this way, I mean you could have been adopted by the Beams. The worst. Imagine learning that you were adopted by the Beams and there was nothing you could do about it."

They didn't really know the name of the couple, but one time when Leslie and Jeanetta had been in the hardware store buying some new towel racks—it was when Jeanetta got her own private bath—they had seen them. A couple was in there buying what was supposed to look like four long wooden beams, only you could tell from across the store that they were Styrofoam that had been painted a gummy dark brown. They were the tackiest-looking things that Leslie and Jeanetta had ever seen. So they followed the man and woman and asked them what they were doing with the "planks," pretending that they thought they were real wood, with him holding four of them on his shoulder with one hand. Anyway, the woman smiled real big and said: "See, John, I told you they looked genuine." And she explained to the girls that they were going to glue them onto the ceiling of their living room to give it a rustic look.

Leslie couldn't get over the Total Awful, as she called it, and so when she wanted to describe something that would be the worst possible thing, she said it belonged to the Beams.

"What if the Beams were my real parents?" Jeanetta asked.

Leslie threw up her hands at the idea; you could tell that was the worst thing she could imagine. "People like that can't be real parents. They glue plastic babies onto the seats of high chairs when grannies come to visit. Come on, Jeanetta Edna Mayfield Foundling Love Child, you dummy, they can't make real babies. When he puts his Styrofoam peter into her plastic place, all they get is artificial flowers. Hey—" She poked at Jeanetta until she laughed.

"Let's take a walk," Leslie commanded. "Let's get out of here. I know Mom has got my room bugged, and she's going to scream the phooey out of us and rummage her finger around to see what we've been up to if we don't get out of here."

The thing was, what you wanted was someone to be serious about it, to understand the genetics of it. Leslie had talked about how good it was that Jeanetta's folks wanted her, but she didn't take into account the main thing: that Jeanetta wasn't the person she thought she was. She'd looked in the mirror all that time and not even seen that she was too stiff to be a cheerleader. And now she looked and didn't know who she was.

At school Monday Leslie passed her a note to Dear Love-Child Foundling, but she didn't let anyone see, as it was still a secret. Jeanetta saw David, too, in the hall, but she walked right by; he was a total stranger to her now.

What she wanted was to see Mr. Jenkins, her biology teacher, as he was the one person who would understand. He had taught them about heredity in the fall, and told them funny things to try out at home, to show that little things that you would never think of as inherited, were. For example, he had them all try to curl their tongues, and the ones who could, he said if they were boys their mothers could, too, and if they were girls their daddies could. It was sex-linked. And then he had them clasp their hands together and look to see which thumb was on top, and if it was the left thumb, then boys and their mothers would do it that way, or girls and their daddies. And the same if it was the right thumb. (The amazing thing was how weird it felt when you clasped your fingers the wrong way and put the other thumb on top.)

Jeanetta had gone home to try out what he told them, the way she guessed that all the students had. But she'd forgotten to do it. Now she wondered if that was foresight on her part, or if it was just that she didn't like to bring up the subject of Mr. Jenkins at home, in case her mother would guess how she felt.

Mr. Jenkins had made heredity very personal, telling them that he was part Scot and part French Huguenot with a touch of Sicilian, and talking about what he got from which ancestor, and she had enjoyed that. It gave you an idea of all those people who came before you, picking out people to love and having children and dying, and it repeating; and it all having to do with the way you looked.

That was the hardest thing about being a foundling: you didn't know where what you saw came from.

Mr. Jenkins could tell her anything she wanted to know about the subject, she was sure of that, because he could have been a famous doctor if he'd gone to medical school. He was that kind of brilliant person who wouldn't ordinarily be teaching in a high school.

She was afraid she couldn't see him alone, because he was popular, and there were always kids hanging around after his classes, and even sometimes after school you'd see someone still talking to him out in the parking lot. But nobody was in his room after school, and she was relieved. She hid back of the door and when he came in she jumped behind him and put her hands over his eyes. She had to reach up really high and so she had to press against him. It made her feel grown up to be that close, and she didn't move until he said: "No fair attacking from behind, Miss Mayfield."

"How did you know it was me?" Maybe he had imagined her breasts leaning against him that way, and so knew exactly how she would feel.

"You're the only midget in the class."

"That's not fair." She jumped up and sat on the side of his desk. "Can I talk to you?"

"I don't know, can you?"

"I mean, are you busy?"

"Not out of the ordinary. You wish to clone a rat?"

"I want to talk about heredity."

"You are thinking of having three green peas?"

42

"Really—" She didn't mind his teasing.

"Fire away." He sat in a student's chair, his long legs sticking out in front of him. He had on moccasins and cords and looked much younger than her daddy, although Leslie had asked him once and she said he was almost as old. He looked like he was in college or an intern or something, except for the lines on his face, but that could be from things not being good at home with his wife.

"Do you think—" she said her words carefully—"that a person is more like his adopted parents on account of having grown up around them, or like his real parents on account of having their genes?" She had rehearsed the question until it sounded very scientific.

"This is an academic question?"

"I was just wondering."

He looked at her like he wondered why she wondered but was being too polite to ask. "Well, now, the honest answer is, beats hell out of me. They've done studies on twins who always turn out to look alike and eat the same food and both be married to girls named Shirley, even when they were separated at age six months and raised in different states. But I've never been sure whether that proves that all twins end up marrying girls named Shirley, or all people who adopt you raise you to be the kind of guy who marries a girl named Shirley. They make the tests prove the answers they start with. But you, Miss Mayfield, probably had in mind such traits as kleptomania and sleepwalking?"

"Would you ever do that?"

"Marry a girl named Shirley? Never."

"Adopt a baby."

"Well, certainly. In fact, I do annually, about twenty every year. I've even taken a liking to midgets from year to year. You plan to put yourself up for adoption and see if you can grow tall with new parents?"

She laughed. He made it all seem silly, but not in a way that made her feel he was making fun of her, or didn't understand the serious side of it. She knew that he must have guessed her secret, but wasn't going to say anything to embarrass her. It would be his way of keeping her confidence.

"Would you do it the other way? Give one away?"

He looked at her closely, and his face looked worried. "I hope I don't know what you're talking about."

"Oh, not me." She blushed. "That's all right. I mean, I'm not having one—" She felt herself look away in pleasure, that he thought of her that way.

"Would I?" He put his legs over the arm of the student chair. "I suppose if it wasn't going to work out for me and some woman, I'd want it at least to work out for the baby." He seemed to be studying her.

"Did you ever?" She knew her voice got almost too low for him to hear. She couldn't help it. It was hard to get so personal.

"Fortunately, no. That wouldn't be an easy matter. But people do it, you know, Jeanetta. Nice people, with guts."

"That's all right—" She couldn't look at him.

He helped her down off the desk. "Any more questions?"

"No." She would have liked to kiss him, but that would have ruined it. She could tell what he was thinking, and that was enough. "Goodbye," she said.

"See you tomorrow, midget," he answered lightly.

She knew that's all he could let himself say.

Walking home, she decided that when she could she would smooth things over with her parents, when there was a natural way; there was no need for them to go around all upset. If they couldn't see that she wasn't the same person she had been, then it just proved that they weren't really her mom and daddy.

Jeanetta and the Deafs

LAST month Leslie and Jeanetta and Pam and the rest of the Jay-Teens had driven to Danville on an overnight trip with their sponsor, who had a friend, Miss Beasley, who was head of volunteers at Kentucky State School for the Deaf. It was part of their community education program: last spring they'd worked with old people at the County Hospital and last fall they'd gone to the Easter Seal Center once a week to help out the generally handicapped.

Miss Beasley had explained to them that most of the kids at the school were born Deafs; and that sometimes Deafs went to schools where they learned to lip-read and sometimes they went to schools where they talked only with sign language, but that here they used Total. Which meant that everyone always talked and signed at the same time and made their faces and bodies do part of the talking, too. The Jay-Teens were part of Total: they helped with Rhythm, Charm, and Sports, the things that Deafs could do with hearing people and not need language. Leslie did Charm, but Jeanetta didn't want anybody to watch her put on makeup, and she wasn't limber enough to do the tumbling part of Sports, so she'd signed up for

Rhythm. Which she thought would be all right, since you couldn't play too loud for Deafs.

Miss Beasley told them that the luckiest Deafs of all were the ones with deaf parents, because these parents knew that the average baby had to hear a word two thousand times before it could say it, and so deaf parents were used to the idea of repetition, and they would say and act out "You want some milk?" "You want some milk?" over and over, and Miss Beasley did the motions with her hands, making a gesture like milking a cow, and all the girls laughed. She said that most hearing parents were embarrassed to talk and sign to infants who they knew couldn't hear, so that those babies didn't know what they'd missed until it was too late to get it. And some never learned what they didn't have.

Jeanetta had liked the Deafs from the start. She had worn her pink sweater and pleated skirt, and a bunch of older girls had gathered around her, and she could tell right off they liked the outfit. They could let you know because you could see their faces and they could see yours.

Last month she had met the eight children that were to be her Rhythm class. They all had on little walkie-talkies that Miss Beasley called Ear Marks, connected to what looked like hearing aids in their ears. To demonstrate how powerful they were, the classroom teacher, called Tripp, had given Jeanetta one and then gone out into the hall, and Jeanetta could still hear her, as if the woman was shouting in her ear, and then she kept on hearing the teacher talking until finally the voice sounded more like a normal conversational tone, and then she heard: "Turn around, I'm outside." And Jeanetta had wheeled around and there was the teacher way out in the yard on the other side of the closed windows. She'd gotten so excited that she'd pointed, and all the little kids ran and looked and waved, and then Miss Beasley told them with her hands and words that the girl in the pink sweater had heard Tripp talking outside.

It was amazing. The Ear Marks were little radios that the children wore all the time; the teacher was the station they listened to. Jeanetta couldn't get over it. What she didn't understand was, if it took so much help to get them to hear something that loud, how they were ever going to hear her play the piano.

Miss Beasley had settled Jeanetta in an office with a box of triangles and a set of drums in one corner, and asked her: "Why do you want to be a high-school helper at K.S.D.?"

"Because I feel bad for all the ones who can't speak and can't hear, and I want to help them learn so they can make something of their lives." She knew she was paraphrasing what they'd been taught in Jay-Teens.

Miss Beasley smiled and asked if Jeanetta had done other volunteer work.

So she told about the Easter Seal Center and then the County Hospital. "I liked that best; it was part of our project to do something for old people. Old people are lonely and they feel better to see some youthful person."

"Here you would be working with youngsters—"

"That's all right."

Today Miss Beasley was explaining to Jeanetta that what they did was called Eurhythmy, which meant moving your body to a beat, and that was how they taught the Deafs to "hear."

48

In the middle of a sentence the director stopped. "Where are you, Jeanetta?"

"I heard you." She felt embarrassed.

"We get accustomed to telling the difference here between getting it and not getting it."

"I was listening—"

"But you were elsewhere. If you'd been deaf I'd have tapped your cheek to let you know I was talking."

"I'm sorry." Jeanetta looked at the woman in the thick gray suit with the thick gray hair. She didn't know what to say. "Last week was my birthday," she explained, the first thing that came to her.

Miss Beasley didn't seem to think that an unusual answer. "Why don't we stop and get a Coke?"

They sat on a sort of bench in the snack area, and Jeanetta, who didn't ordinarily drink Cokes because it was bad for your complexion, had one, and the strong stinging taste helped.

Miss Beasley sat and didn't say anything. It was odd, but it must be that if you worked with Deafs all the time you got used to not saying anything unless you needed to.

Which must be the influence which made Jeanetta blurt out: "I'm adopted. I just found out."

"How does it feel?"

As soon as she heard the question Jeanetta knew that that was what she'd been trying to answer since her mom and daddy had told her about picking her out from the rest.

"It feels—" She turned and looked at gray Miss Beasley and began to sob. "It feels like Santa Claus."

It was Total Awful, as Leslie would say, to sit there in the Deafs' snack bar crying and not being able to stop.

That was it. When her mom and daddy told her, she knew that something about hearing it had happened to her before. It was when she was in second grade. She had just started taking piano and Miss Crispin was helping her to control her wanting to bang at the top of her strength, teaching her how to be softer, telling her that you didn't hit a keyboard the way you did a punching bag. Jeanetta had just started taking music and she loved it. Then some big kids at recess told her that Santa was your mom and dad and that only little creeps didn't know that, little babies who wrote lists to Santa when all the time it was your parents figuring out how to use their charge accounts.

She had asked her mom when she got home, and Mom had told her about the letter to Virginia and the spirit of Christmas and Jeanetta hadn't been able to believe it. She had asked her daddy and he had said his flowery words to her for at least five minutes. She couldn't believe it: that they had lied to her.

Next time she was at Miss Crispin's for a lesson she had demanded: "What else?"

"What else what, Jeanetta? Don't shout."

"*What else?*" She had got red in the face and screamed and banged, a seven-year-old who did not want to believe what she was told.

Miss Crispin, a little woman who never lost her temper, said, "There are many fairy tales and myths." Something like that. She'd calmed Jeanetta down with a handful of cookies, and for Christmas had given her a copy of *The Wizard of Oz*, which her parents were surprised at, but thought it was a nice thing to do. Jeanetta knew that Miss Crispin had been trying to say that Santa was like the Wizard. But he wasn't. He wasn't the same at all.

Later, when Leslie got to be her best friend in fourth

grade, she asked her: "What else?" because Leslie knew everything, and Leslie had said, being very grown-up, "God."

But that wasn't the same. Santa wasn't like God. God was something that you could have ideas about the way you did about gravity without knowing what was really true. You heard about God at church, but that was just the Reverend E. Mack Jones and his version, and then you had the ideas of your Sunday School teachers, and they were all different. It was the same as speakers at assembly, when you could think that they had their way of looking at life and you had yours.

Last week Reverend Mack had talked the way he always did about Jesus, trying to make Jesus as handy as your hammer and as nearby as your CB radio, as he was always saying.

He talked about a scientist he had seen on TV, named Carl Sagan, who, he said, "makes a terrible mistake dismissing theology with a brushoff. That's because, despite his claims of understanding the whole of the universe, he doesn't set out by the garage like you and me and try to penetrate the heavens. So that he never comes to the good news that Jesus is the Source and the Glue in the middle that tolds our whole cosmos together. That's because he has never stopped to think about the basic fact that we know that Jesus can be trusted, because Jesus is God in skin."

That was one person's idea, and your not agreeing with that didn't mean anything about God, but something about the Reverend E. Mack Jones and what a Beam he was.

But somebody like a minister telling you what he sincerely believed wasn't in any way the same as your mom and daddy lying to you about something that they knew wasn't so. Which was the case with Santa, and her being adopted.

"First they pretend its *not* your parents," she almost screamed, "and then you find out they've just pretended all along that they *are* your mom and daddy."

Miss Beasley didn't say anything.

"I'm sorry," Jeanetta whispered, her face wet and smeared from rubbing her eyes.

"Natural parents also pretend to be someone who can give you everything you want."

"They don't lie."

"Of course they do, in hundreds of ways."

"I don't believe it."

Miss Beasley finished her Coke.

"You don't know, you don't have children—"

"I was one, in my time."

Jeanetta struck out at her, for not understanding. "How come you never got married?"

"Because women can't marry women."

"Oh." Jeanetta blushed.

"Tripp will have the students ready." Miss Beasley got up and buttoned her gray jacket and smoothed her gray hair. Looking sharply at Jeanetta, she said: "It's time for us to get started."

Tripp brought the eight children to the doorway of the Rhythm room. She was talking away to Miss Beasley, but also moving her hands for the kids. "I told them we were going to see the girl who came before and heard me in the yard. And thank you, dear—" she turned to Jeanetta—"for wearing the same pink sweater. See, she has on a pink sweater." She did her hands. "And that we were going to hear music. I told them that three times and then Doobie asks me, 'Are we going to gym?' Doobie, you're a bird-brain." She twirled her fingers and tapped his head, and then she and Miss Beasley laughed and the other kids laughed and made the same motion, and Doobie looked happy and did it, too. It was clear he was a favorite, and Tripp explained that he was the only one in class who had Deafs for parents, which made all the difference.

The way Tripp motioned with her hand to Doobie's head gave you the idea of scatterbrain or out-to-lunch or loony; Jeanetta's grandmother used to do the same kind of thing when she said someone was "daft." And Jeanetta had understood what that meant when she was very little, before she had any idea what the word meant, from the way her grandmother did the gesture and then laughed. That must be how it was with the Deafs: they got the idea of it, even if they didn't get the words.

She followed Miss Beasley's gray suit into the room where a piano sat on a wooden platform. The box of triangles was there and a set of drums and some other oblong boxes that played the scale when you hit them with a rod.

The children had been told about the piano and what the idea was, but they had never "heard" one before. Miss Beasley helped them pull a couple of wood benches over on each side of the big baby grand, and climb up, four on each side. "You will want to take off your shoes, Jeanetta. That way you can feel the beat through your feet, more or less the way the children will with their hands and faces."

She then told Doobie and the rest to kneel on the benches and place their hands palm down on top of the piano, and then their cheeks.

"I'm going to leave you with them for a few minutes," she said. "It will make you more relaxed, and if I stay they'll watch me for cues. If you need us, Tripp and I will be right outside in the hall. Play what you like, whatever you brought with you, and don't mind if they jump around or talk to each other. Next time, if you like, I'll work with you on soft and loud, fast and slow, and we can get them to sing with you, la la la." While she talked to Jeanetta she talked at the same time to the kids, touching the piano, demonstrating soft and loud and fast and slow as she said the words.

"I haven't played in a long time." Jeanetta felt scared.

"It isn't as if they have a basis for comparison, is it?"

Jeanetta looked at them. Doobie was next to her, popping up and down. Bird-brain, she said to herself, get with it.

Miss Beasley said afterward that Jeanetta had played for thirty minutes without stopping. That she hadn't known the kids were even there. That they could hear her all the way to the administration building, and that some of the partial hearing had been able to pick up the beat in their wing next door. That when she returned, Doobie and his seven classmates were still bent over the piano. Some had sat down to get more comfortable, and they'd lifted their faces up to watch Jeanetta.

"They could hear you across the whole campus," Miss Beasley said.

"Bird-brain." Jeanetta whirled her hand and tapped her head. "This always happens to me." She was embarrassed.

But Miss Beasley looked pleased and not mad. And Tripp, who was standing with her, shoving the kids out into the hall, talking to them and waving her hands, looked like she didn't mind at all.

54

"You showed them what all our words can't do," Miss Beasley told her. "What music is for the hearing."

"Did I?"

"You did. You made quite an impression."

As she walked Jeanetta to the assembly room she said, "The college I went to is having a summer program in the arts. You might enjoy it."

"Leslie's mother made her promise she wouldn't go anywhere this summer."

"You're not Leslie, are you?"

That night she let her mom and daddy tuck her in bed, the way they used to.

"You doing all right, JeanEddie?" her daddy asked.

"Sure, Daddy."

"If there's any problem, I want it to be handled."

"There's no problem."

"I know it'll dispute some people's opinion of the matter, but we waited to tell you until we judged it to be the right occasion."

Her mom looked hurt that she didn't know what was in Jeanetta's head anymore, but she pulled up the yellow checked spread and said, "We were afraid we shouldn't have told you the way we did."

"Oh, Mom," she said, "it didn't make any difference. You and Daddy have always been like Santa Claus to me."

Jeanetta

S L O W L Y she took off her clothes in front of the birthday mirrors. She had the light down dim and the radio was playing John Denver. She looked at herself and it was like she saw the girl for the first time: whose eyes were those, whose nose, whose hair, whose tongue that curled, whose fingers that clasped left thumb over right? Whose breasts?

She imagined a young woman who looked like her, maybe a receptionist or lab technician, someone who worked for the doctor and saw him every day. That would be the natural way for it to happen, for them to fall in love. He would try to get her to leave, not to get hurt. She would promise that she would not make trouble, that she only wanted to love him for a little while. He would argue with her that he was married, he was not a person to do that. But, in the end, because he was in love with her, they would become lovers.

Maybe it had to be over when she knew she was pregnant. Or maybe that's what made it over. The realization of what they had done. He would offer, being a doctor, to get rid . . . No. He wouldn't allow that. He would say: "I want our baby to have a happy life. I want to have a child by you who will live part of our life for us."

And they would cling to each other and her heart would break but she wouldn't let on, and he would try to stay in control but he would break down, too.

They would both go away to other places. To start new lives. Apart.

Leaving behind the baby to carry on their love.

(When she shut her eyes the doctor looked like Mr. Jenkins.)

In this way the girl began to imagine a new Jeanetta.

2

Harry

———————◆———————

A т least that's the way I reconstructed her story later, after I met her, and the Life Underwriter, and his wife, Betty Sharp Mayfield.

The way the girl imagined the events before her birth was not, of course, the way they were; but that may be true for all of us. At any rate, in her case I can be sure, as I was there at the start, involved with her real parents in another sort of adoption: mine of them. At that time I was a vain, foppish, fraudulent nineteen-year-old, sorely in search of a surrogate family. My shame was that I came from parents who could christen a son Harry James and have no inkling the name had a familiar ring; my hope, that the world would take to heart my newly created self, Harrod Roncevaux.

Aspen in June in 1965 was paradise. We gathered for breakfast at the Epicure—everyone with knapsack, rolled tent, or music case—our homes on our backs. We ate our butter-drenched croissants as sweet-faced Huskies and great creamy Samoyeds waited, untethered, in the chill outside air, and a light snow fell, hung a minute on the brilliant blooms along old fences, heightening their colors deeper and truer than any I had ever seen, then glistened in the sun and melted.

The Music School still hovered between new quarters in the lush meadows on the way to the layered red mountains called Maroon Bells and its old location in the small Victorian town; so that you could still hear musicians tuning up, the sound of strings carrying out of upstairs windows into the clear morning air.

I could not imagine a more perfect world.

Except that, needless to say, the musicians never noticed it.

The main thing you have to learn about musicians is that they do not inhabit their bodies; rather, they live in the boxes and pipes they play upon. You can tell this by listening: they have hypochondria of the instrument. The same way that you hear old folks talking about the fret they're having with their colon, duodenum, or esophagus, herniated disc or creaking arthritis, you get musicians on their mediums. The violinists, of which I was trying to be one, talked incessantly of the plague of centrally heated houses in the winter which caused their beloved instruments to sound harsh and gritty, and the equal curse of damp and heavy summers whose humidity made their violins sullen and unresponsive. It was like women talking of their periods, this constant sharing of swelling up and drying out.

You can tell this about musicians just by looking. They are constructed in a weird way, most of them having little tops and great big bottoms and sort of vacant, stringy faces. They are a loosely assembled collection of appendages, lips and fingers, waiting to fasten on to wood and gut and reed to come to life.

I didn't blame myself for being mixed up with such companions. It was no more than you could expect to happen to someone growing up in a family where both parents are dead ringers for Rose Kennedy. My dad, naturally, had man's hair, and wore those black cloth professorial jackets, and my mother had a man's haircut, too, but it was puffed out over the forehead for gender identification, and she wore those black skirts and leotard tops that women who carry placards wear. I'm not sure what it was that gave the Rose Kennedy resemblance, something about one eye being a little bit somewhere else, and the way of leaning the head and hiking the shoulders, and a pinched upper-class look. But I've only seen her in photographs. The point was, in some way they were identical. There weren't a lot of cues to read in their faces or gestures to distinguish one from the other.

Growing up, I thought that was how adults looked: big and identical. The way some people think of babies as small and alike. Naturally, when I got to school and saw all these folks called teachers who looked different, I didn't know where to start to figure things out.

My gravitation to musicians was inevitable. As the child of Liberals, I had a duty to ally myself with misfits. And in those days I went along with all expectations: was a musical prodigy, had a burning desire to dissect frogs in the kitchen sink, and forgot to brush my teeth. But my heart wasn't in it.

(Once, when I was in junior high school, we were taken on a tour of the eleemosynaries, as we called them, and when we got to the School for the Blind I had this nagging sense of familiarity. It wasn't until I got home that I realized it was like being at the Junior String Project with the musicians. They couldn't see, so they got it all by feel:

63

they groped along, coming alive only at the touch of the Other with their hands and mouths.)

Not coming by this transference naturally, I had passed in the string recitals and here at the Music School by dint of making my whole body the instrument, rather than the other way around. My chin clamping down on the wood, my left hand holding on for dear life against the whipping of my right hand, set us all to vibrating like a tuning fork. The violin lay there, neither swollen nor dry, while Harry played himself.

June in Aspen was too lovely to spend with musicians, and I had found a true friend: a yellow dog who came from one of the houses on the edge of town, at the base of Ajax Mountain, in whose shadow we lived. Every day, after hot tea and rolls at the Epicure, I would take the short (forty-five minutes if you were in shape) local hike up Ute Trail to the top of a small overlook, a knee of Ajax, two thousand feet above the town. Yellow Dog, a young, frisky bitch, would race ahead of me up the steep switchbacks that left me panting; she would dash off and run back, egging me on, showing me that four legs, even on a puppy, beat the hell out of two, even in their prime.

At the top she would sit beside me, flank to flank, on a wedge of space on the top of the rocky promontory, where we sipped from my canteen of water and munched a roll saved from breakfast. And squinted down at the tiny model of paradise below.

I told her everything. I explained about the musicians; she said she never mixed with them herself. We talked a lot in those first weeks and she let me get it all out of my system. I promised that one day we would make it out to the higher, longer trails, American and Cathedral, those that went through the aspen and then the firs to reach the glacial lakes squeezed in the high crevices of the Rockies.

At that time in Aspen, if you had the money, you ate dinner at the Copper Kettle, which gave you a full seven courses, from soup to Stilton, for a fixed price of $8.50. As the age for drinking was twenty-one and a lot of us weren't, you also had to have along a seasoned elder to order the wine.

Before these dinners we provided our reason for being there: the Music Festival Concerts. Those of us who did not solo played Stravinsky, Hindemith, Prokofiev, and Poulenc with the Festival Orchestra. Usually we were backup for the Netherlands Quartet—two violins, a viola, and a cello— or Walter Susskind on piano, as these were the main show-pieces. In those days each performance had vocalists as well, to fill out our twilight serenades as we worked our way through the summer with a Modern Program, a French Program, a German Program, an Evening of Chamber, a Night of Beethoven. (My own favorite composer we per-formed only once, the Hungarian Zoltán Kodály. He was still alive that magical summer, and I used to imagine that he appeared in the audience to hear us play his work.)

After we ate at the Copper Kettle or some lesser spot, the concert-goers, for whom we existed, opened their sum-mer homes to us. At that time I didn't have a lot to do with the men, not sure how to take the occasional drunken lapse in which a hand lingered too long on my shoulder, or a knee pressed against mine in the heat of a close conversation on the sofa. The women I did better with, at least those damask types who had had lovers, and homes and gardens, and disappointing children, and husbands who were both philanderers and philanthropists, and who could say, with a certain smile, that they had reached an age where they had come to value the durability of Aubusson rugs. They thought me trustworthy, seeing perhaps deeper into me than I saw into myself—after all, they had grandsons.

That was how it was then: the bright, snow-brushed mornings, the afternoons of practice and rehearsal, the nights in the amphitheater sending sweet music up into the air of heaven. An Eden spoiled only by its inhabitants.

Danny and Ebie Wister stood out from all the rest that first morning at the Epicure. I thought them—him with his close-cropped hair and brown tweed suit, her with her flowered dress and dark, straight locks—the most normal-looking couple I had ever seen.

That was what caught my attention initially; that and the fact that he could make a scene in public and get over it so fast. Here was this man at an outside table lambasting the waitress because his coffee had no cream and his rolls had no butter. Then, with restitution, came serenity. His anger forgotten, he ate with gusto.

I was drawn to that sudden calm like a moth to the flame.

(There was on TV at that time a commercial for Tums or something in which there was this line drawing of a fat man who looked like Alfred Hitchcock, and inside his stomach were squalls and hurricanes and lightning; and then the Tums or whatever would be dropped in, and all would change abruptly to a tranquil pond on which a little boat bobbed calmly on these little lapping waves. I never missed whatever show came on, just to see that storming stomach subside into a benign scene.)

It is hard in retrospect to explain how I got the nerve to go out to them and sit myself down at their table. Part of it had to do with general loneliness; part with the crumbs

I had received at home. The morning that I pulled a metal chair across the gravel to their table, keeping an eye on my violin case and canteen left behind inside, my only fear was that I would end up where I was already. The promise of a little gain gave me the nerve to drop my casual opening comment: "You don't look like musicians."

"We're not," the woman answered.

"She used to be," he countered.

"The boy doesn't mean that, Danny. These people play in concert. . . ."

I could have left right then; they would have gone on all day, as the sun warmed the air and opened the flowers trailing over the latticed fence. They would have gone on arguing, with him tugging at her sleeve, not letting go, and her squinting in that way as if she looked past us all at what was coming down the road.

But I didn't leave. Which is how they came into my life.

"How's the coffee?" I asked, to have something to say.

He looked at his empty cup. He twisted her sleeve.

"We've had better," she answered, looking past the wrought-iron tables and their umbrellas. "Are you a musician, then? Do you play an instrument?"

"Violin." I was grateful to prolong the conversation.

"Did you leave it in there?" She peered through the open doorway.

"I just stepped out for a moment—" I must have flushed.

"Won't they take it?"

"They won't notice; they're musicians."

The man had light blue eyes, very light, which seemed strange in his rather swarthy face. He was lower-class, I found myself noting, unable to help it. (That was part of the curse of coming from the Roses K.: Liberals are the first to note how far their *noblesse* is reaching down to *oblige.*) Was she also? I couldn't tell. She wasn't Aubusson rugs, and she didn't look like the mothers of my classmates; I had not even minimal cues to decide. When they wore black, big-sleeved, flowered dresses wholly out of style, rouge on an otherwise white face, no lipstick, and had that way of gazing off, you couldn't tell. It could be either end of the scale.

"We're Dan and Ebie Wister," she introduced them.

"Harrod Roncevaux," I answered. Surely my voice cracked. How fake my fake name sounded, said right out like that.

"Harold?" Danny reached out a handshake.

"Harrod," she corrected him. "Like Harrodsburg, at home."

"Ebie?" I asked her.

"E.B. Think of it that way."

"Where's Harrodsburg?"

"Western Kentucky. We're from Paducah. Nowadays, anyway."

Danny laughed. "I was going to tell him up the road a piece. I forgot; we're not there, we're here." He laughed again. "You'll have to pardon me, Harold. My head is full of uranium. It's paid to be, these days."

I looked at his big head with its mowed-off hair and imagined it weighed down with heavy ore. It was a good image.

I smiled at him.

In response, he brightened up, and confided loudly, "She's expecting." He leaned the load of uranium against her hair.

"Danny—he's seen a pregnant woman before."

I'm not sure I had, except in the movies, but I said, "That's nice." What I was thinking was that she must be almost my mother's age and what was she doing having a baby? And I remember I also thought, Where is it?, because there was no sign of any kind. If anything, her middle seemed concave.

"Harrod—" She turned to me and looked closely, and I could see way back into her head but not really into her eyes. "Are you staying at a place where we could make coffee? We're in a motel which—"

I did not figure out that morning where she was leading the three of us. At that time I assumed they needed what they said they did: a place to fix a homemade cup. Later, I calculated that she must have read my face at once and guessed what I did not know myself: that I was ready to give my heart, at least the filial part, to Danny.

"Sure," I said. "Four blocks away, that's all. Sure." I leaped up so fast my metal chair fell backward on the gravel. "I have a Chemex." (The fact was I didn't drink coffee; I'd bought the pot only in case I ever needed to impress anyone, and a pound of ground espresso to go with it. I had also bought two novels by Dostoyevsky and all seven volumes of Proust. Which I had never opened. They were to throw around on the bed and floor. And a cheap paperback copy of some book called *She* by H. Rider Haggard, which I had got at a book sale, and which I imagined added an esoteric touch. I got it because I envied his name, and had even thought of doing something with it: H. Rider Roncevaux, H. Harrod Haggard, something along those lines.)

I lived in a rented A-frame that faced southwest and, in the afternoon, especially in the loft where the bed was, became an oven; but it would be cool enough now, early in the day. I tried to remember if I had left the place clean. The sheets would be more or less on the floor where I'd left them, but Danny and Ebie wouldn't be going up there, as you had to climb a ladder. The living room–kitchen downstairs would be fine, with its books strewn about and a studied arrangement of leaves from my hikes stuck in my spare canteen on the table.

Then it dawned on me that there wasn't any cream, which was what Danny had bawled the waitress out for forgetting. There was only one thing to do. In what I hoped was a casual thiefly manner, I picked up the cream pitcher and stuck it in my windbreaker pocket, holding it upright from the inside.

As they gathered their things, she, looking quite agreeable, nodded and picked up the sugar bowl and put it in her purse. When they got up to go, she kept on rising until she and that black flowered dress were almost to my shoulders, and I could not see a baby bulge anywhere. But Danny quit getting up, which is to say I thought he must be walking on his knees; and then I saw that while we were the same height sitting down, standing up he was almost a foot shorter. He must have forgot to grow legs. I wondered if his tailor took those brown tweed suits and made two pair of pants out of each pair of trousers, since he only needed half the length.

"Get your violin, Harrod," Ebie said. "Give me the cream." And she led us in her floaty way right through the Epicure to get my things and out the side door onto the street—where gentle-faced Huskies waited in the bright, cool, bloom-scented air.

They had both read all ten books strewn about my living room.

"You remember when I read *She*?" Ebie asked him. "That foolish thing. I told you I thought it must actually have been written by Edgar Rice Burroughs."

70

"I cried at the end of *The Brothers Karamazov*," Danny confided to me. He held the book in hands which looked as battered as the book did new. "When that old daddy crumbles the bread on the coffin. I bet I could recite that scene by heart, to this day."

"That's because," Ebie said, "you thought it was set in West Virginia."

"Didn't see anywhere that said it wasn't."

They sat on the rented studio couch, lightly touching all the time.

I served my first mugs of Chemex coffee with what I hoped was the proper nonchalance, wishing there was something besides the landlord's brown-and-green service. At least we had cream and sugar.

Danny looked around. "Nice place."

"It gets hot in the afternoon."

"But you can pull the curtains, can't you, across the front?" Ebie looked at the glass.

"Upstairs in the loft is hot."

"The mountains wind around south of us here, don't they?" Danny studied the layout, got his bearings, and then relaxed. "This is the first good cup of coffee we've had since we got here."

"Chemex takes the credit," I said modestly.

"Won't you play for us?" Ebie had flipped open my novels one at a time, and seen that the pages had not even been opened all the way, much less marked. I felt that she was now suggesting that perhaps the violin, too, was a prop. That made me angry. Carrying as it did the slight sting of truth.

"What would you like?" I got up and began the operation of tuning up. I could call her bluff. If she used to play all the time the way that Danny said, she could at least

71

name one piece. I expected her to say "The Flight of the Bumblebee."

"It's difficult to breathe up here, the altitude," she murmured. "We're not used to it yet." She looked vague. "Brahms? Mozart? Whatever you have music for."

It was true I could play nothing without the notes before me, but I didn't let that faze me. I played part of a concerto by Goldmark, certain she would never have heard it and therefore have no comparison. I was not bad; I was no maestro, and something of both fire and technique was lacking, but I was not bad.

"I like that." Ebie shut her eyes and seemed a lot more present than she did when she was talking to you.

"That was a fine piece," Danny said. "My old daddy used to play the fiddle, when he was able." He was silent a minute, then asked, "Anybody ever call you Harry?"

I blanched at the sound of my real name. "Never," I lied. "Not ever."

"Ebie used to play," Danny went on, paying no attention to my disclaimer.

"Harrod's not interested in all that." She reminded him of his manners.

He was back to thinking about the past. "We lost a little girl, Harold, and Ebie never played again, not a note. I figured, with this one coming, she might take it up again."

"If I'm not playing when the baby comes, then I won't have to stop playing if something goes wrong. You don't make any allowance for the fact that I'm forty years old and have no business having another."

"Time you did. She died; you didn't. The piano didn't." He turned to me. "It's a nine-foot Steinway we've got." Then back to her. "Music didn't die, damn it. You'll mark this baby with your talk before it even gets out on the delivery table."

"You want me to have this one because you want Bea back, and she isn't coming back."

They were shouting at each other, still inches apart on the landlord's couch.

"You're crazy as your kin. You should never have gone back to that swamp. Every time you set foot in that god-forsaken house with those Grade A lunatics something goes wrong."

Ebie's voice got tight. "There's only one loon left."

"Good riddance. I don't want your mama back and I wish your old man would join her." He was back in a rage, the way he had been at the Epicure, but magnified. His face was beet red. "I'd murder your old daddy if I could get past his lunatic barricade of unpaid tax forms."

"You think I'll go back."

"You will, I know it in my bones. You got this one on the way, and that lunatic will cough blood or whatever it takes, and you'll forget everything that happened the last time, and go running back. Same as you did with your mama."

"You're saying I killed Bea, you always say that. It takes the sting out for you." She drew in her breath. "It was all right for you to drive three hundred miles every weekend to carry your withered daddy outside in the backyard and turn around and drive three hundred miles back. It was all right for us to move to Paducah and breathe coal dust so you could make the trip to *your* daddy." She looked away.

"It was," Danny said. "It was owed."

He put his hand on her stomach then, and left it there until his color faded, his fury subsiding as quickly as it had come. He kept his hand on her caved-in middle until he was mild again: a rainbow and a sailboat on a still pond.

This fighting went on between them until the end of their days together, but I did not understand its origins or inevitability at the start. The facts of their lives and the nature of the recurring dispute over parity to fathers—that Danny's was for many years a helpless stroke victim in the black mountains of West Virginia, that hers was an equally incapacitated nut locked up in a back room in rural Louisiana—did not soak in until the winter I spent with them in Paducah, Kentucky. At the time of that argument in my rented A-frame in Aspen all that made an impression on me was the amazing fact that they could shout out such personal attacks on one another in front of a comparative stranger, and then touch, and let it go.

It was the contrast that got to me. The Roses K., you see, could hold a grudge as long as they had breath to draw, and never let out a hint of it.

In those days I took delight in telling the concert-goers in Aspen that I had lost my father in the bombing of Guernica. I liked to do that because most of them were from New York and they knew nothing of Guernica except that Picasso had noted it, so they had to look distressed, and convey how sorry they were that my old man had been a victim of Cubism. (That wasn't when I lost him, naturally; at the time of the bombing, in 1937, he was a twenty-one-year-old student in Michigan, and I was nowhere in sight.)

The point was I never lost either of my parents, as I never had them in the first place. Certain causes had beat me to their attention by a full two decades. My dad, Wendell, lived and fed on his hatred of Franco's Spaniards: "Oppressors who build their temples on the gnawed bones of separatists"—to pick a line at random from his anger. He had allied himself in his mind with one particular group of the oppressed, the Basques, whom he had traced all the way back to a mountain clan that defeated Charlemagne at Roncevaux. (I had thought of changing my name to Harry Charlemagne, but that seemed a little obvious, even for musicians.)

With equal obsession, my mom, Marie, hated Unfair Labor Practices. At the time I met the Wisters we were living in Texas, where my dad was teaching at the university and working on learning the dying Basque language, Euzkara, and my mom was picketing the big landholders in the Rio Grande Valley. She and a group of like-minded women worked with the unions who had helped organize the grape-pickers of California, and who were going to do the same thing for the melon farmers of Texas. (I remember wondering if there was some connection between fruit and Unfair Practices, or if there could also be Okra Protests and Collard Collectives. In other words, if it had to be something you liked to eat to make the boycott worthwhile, the way church-goers thought it cheating if you gave up spinach for Lent.)

At any rate, while other mothers contented their consciences by picketing the supermarkets with big placards which read: SABROSA MELONS PRODUCED BY UNFAIR LABOR STANDARDS, my mom took part in the trek known as the Labor Day March. The idea was that the canteloupe farmers were to walk all the way from the Rio Grande Valley to the State Capitol in Austin—a distance I remember as right at three hundred miles—to tell the Governor to his face that they had their rights. Naturally, Mom decided that she had to make the walk with the protestors, to show that she gave more than lip-service to the cause.

So, last year, for the month of August Mom trudged the highway—being passed every day by these fast trucks piled with melons, like camels with loads on their backs—across the unirrigated stretch of South Texas. Not surprisingly, she got home sick as a dog, going to bed with exhaustion and pneumonia, and, therefore, not able to be present when the Governor of Texas failed to meet the marchers on the Capitol steps and they all turned around and rode the bus home.

I had fantasies that as she lay in dehydrated delirium I force-fed her a whole Sabrosa melon. But not Rose K. pater. His response when she collapsed into bed was: nothing. He pursed his lips and translated his Euzkara, and did not vent himself on the fruitlessness of such ventures.

"I suppose you're glad," she whispered to him.

"Don't project," he said.

"You thought it was foolish, didn't you?" Her face looked hot.

"You did what you considered right."

"What did you do while I was gone?"

"Read, and wrote, as usual." He edged toward the door.

"You could at least bring me some tea."

"Hot or iced?" he asked, without inflection.

That being the biggest confrontation I ever heard between my parents, is it any wonder I attached myself at once to Dan and Ebie Wister?

"You've got a nice place here, Harold," he said, handing me his empty mug for a refill.

"Harrod," Ebie corrected him automatically. "Like Harrodsburg."

"No kin," I said.

76

She raised her brows slightly, and a look of complicity passed between us.

"What're you doing out here in Aspen?" I asked Danny.

"Physics Institute," he said.

And I kicked myself for not having guessed that from the head-full-of-uranium-ore business. I knew they sometimes had scientists as well as executives and the like out for brainstorming sessions.

He told me how he had studied at Chicago, and did I know that Fermi, who orchestrated the first controlled nuclear reaction, had done so under the stadium at Chicago? Then he told me that he used to be at Los Alamos, but that for the last ten-plus years he'd been in Paducah, Kentucky, at the A.E.C.'s uranium-processing plant, because his old daddy had been sick.

I wondered if doing it under the stadium meant they couldn't afford a proper lab in those days, but I, being in my stupid phase, hesitated to ask. "Physics, huh?" was all I said.

"They've put us at the Meadows," Ebie said, helping me out. "Danny hates it. He hates to eat out. The food isn't bad; it's that it isn't what we're used to."

I couldn't imagine a woman in that dress in a kitchen. It was like atoms exploding in a football stadium: if you haven't seen it you can't conceive of it. In my experience women in aprons in kitchens appeared only in school readers. What did she fix? Soup? Lima beans? That made me smile in spite of myself: Roncevaux had a meager imagination.

"What can't you get to eat?" I pried a little, unable to guess.

"It's the way you fix it that becomes habit. Here the

vegetables are too raw and the meat is too done and the salads are coated in dressing. The cold things are lukewarm and the hot things are cold." She looked off, in her way. "Danny makes a scene."

He tugged at her again. "Well," he said, "it costs three times what it should and tastes like slop. What do you expect?"

"Next year if we come again, we'll rent a kitchenette." But she didn't sound as if she had any confidence about the existence of next year.

"I have a hotplate," I offered, as it was in plain sight, wondering if that was what they'd been fishing for.

"Do you?" She made the first real smile I'd seen, and looked at me thoughtfully, right in the eyes.

"That would be mighty nice." Danny beamed in anticipation.

"I don't know what you can cook on a hotplate," I said, because what I'd had done on it was nothing, as I ate all my meals out or did cold cheese and bread when the money was going too fast. For that matter, I had no notion what you could do on a full kitchen range.

"Could we bring something and fix supper, then?" Ebie looked at once pleased and relieved. "What is your schedule?" She had risen to her feet as if to shop at once.

"I'm through the concert at eight. But you can come earlier if you want. I can leave it unlocked."

"That sure would be nice," Danny said. He looked at Ebie. "If you get a skillet you could do a stew."

"And fry some green tomatoes." She warmed visibly. "Maybe make a griddle cake with blueberries for dessert. They tell us this is a garden state, with produce trucked in every day."

Danny looked as if he might cry. "We could get some

decent coffee again before the nighttime stuff starts in."
He turned to me. "I have to be there ready to go at eight
myself. You'll have to come hear us sound forth one of
these nights when you're free. Dull stuff, but there's always
a lot of disagreement in the audience, knockdown-dragout
stuff from people who don't know what they're talking
about. Lively anyway."

"We'll miss you, then, if you're not through before
eight." Ebie seemed concerned, but her need to please
Danny was stronger than her urge for propriety.

What I should have done, naturally, which never even
dawned on me, was to put the hotplate in their hands to
take to their motel. I guess I wanted them there in my
A-frame.

(But she must have known that, too. As well as where
to buy ten hotplates of her own.)

"We don't perform every night," I said. "Some nights
I'm free." Thinking I could cut a rehearsal without a backward glance.

"Don't go to trouble, Harold," Danny said. "But it
would sure be a treat for us, for a change."

"You can call me Harry," I choked out. "My dad does."
Forgetting totally, in the warmth of the moment, that I
had denied the name such a short time ago.

Danny and Ebie did come and use my hotplate that
first night, and saved me some corn fritters. They seemed
to think you could cook anything you wanted in a skillet
on one burner. The next time they did potato pancakes.
She grated a lot of raw potatoes and onion up and added
a little flour and egg and fried it up real fast, and I thought
it was wonderful. She didn't find green tomatoes in the
market, so she fried slices of lemon with the chicken the

first time, and with pork chops the second. She wanted to make a turnip pie, as she called it, but I wasn't too sad that there weren't any turnips available either. Anyway, in a couple of weeks, when he didn't have to be back at the Institute, they took me out to dinner at the Copper Kettle as repayment.

We ate the whole seven courses, down to our pears and cheese after the chocolate mousse, all accompanied by two bottles of French wine. I was thrilled to finally get there without the company of musicians; but to tell the truth the food didn't hold a candle to the potato pancakes on the hotplate. Which was an eyeopener for me, Harrod.

The dinner cost a lot, for those days, but they didn't seem to mind. They paid the bill with none of the guilt over self-indulgence I was used to in the Roses K.

When we were back in my A-frame, Ebie asked: "Why don't you come stay with us, Harry, when I have the baby? Danny will be lonesome. He doesn't like to stay by himself."

I had just navigated serving hot mugs of Chemex coffee, which I did now as if I had been born to it. "I go to school in California," I answered, not meaning that anything at Santa Cruz could keep me from it, but hoping to get some idea when she was talking about, as at this point the baby looked to be something they were inventing.

"Do you go in January?" she helped me out.

"No, I think we get most of the month off. It's the quarter system." I spoke firmly, not having any idea if either fact was true. My arrangement with college was in many ways as nebulous as that with my parents.

"Then why not come? We'll let you earn your board and keep."

Danny was twisting her hair like mad at that point,

reminded that she would need to go off again, to have it, and that nothing good ever came of that.

The idea appealed to me a lot. I imagined myself looking after Danny the same way that he had done for his father, saying later when I recounted it in some detail that it was owed. It was clear he'd need somebody. The baby would be little and wouldn't count; Ebie would be busy tending to it all the time.

"Sure," I said. "I mean, I guess I can."

"Should we write your parents?" Ebie looked at me with a glancing smile, and the idea crossed my mind that she knew all about how unnecessary that was.

I imagined the two Rose Kennedys in their black cloth outfits, their sharp noses focused down at their respective desks. I had an image of them in my mind, sitting back to back, in straight chairs. In that image they faced out opposite windows, she watching the Marchers and he watching the Basques. Neither saying a word.

As a matter of fact, they were seldom home and never available. I couldn't even imagine a scenario in which I asked their permission. I'd leave a note tucked under the magnet on the refrigerator: *Gone to Paducah. Back in a few years. Harry James, your son.*

"No problem," I said calmly. "Don't bother."

"Do you drive?"

"What?" That confused me. I had a sudden vision of tractors or coal carts or something, not having an idea what that part of the world looked like.

"Drive a car."

"Sure."

"I don't anymore," Ebie said.

That seemed impossible. I thought everyone did, unless they were deciding to walk three hundred miles in the

August sun in tennis shoes. I mean, maybe she was a nut, too, one of the kind that doesn't believe in technology, married to somebody who smashes atoms. In accelerated schools we call that irony.

"It would be a help," Ebie said. "I won't want to be walking, at the last. While Danny's at work . . ." By then he was twisting her sleeve almost to a rag.

"Why don't you drive?" I asked her.

"I used to." She let it go at that.

"Well, sure. Be glad to."

She considered that settled, and moved on. "When does the Music Festival finish? We'd like to come hear you play."

"It goes all summer."

"Good, then, you pick a night for us."

"My old daddy used to play the fiddle," Danny said. "When he was able."

After they had gone home to Kentucky, Yellow Dog and I talked the matter over. She came when I whistled, as every day, bounding out from the trees by the last house on the edge of town. She bit at the bright air and said that when you were young you could do anything, and stretched, and raced ahead, and then barreled back, skidding into my legs, eager to hear all about my invitation to visit the Wisters.

At the top, side by side, we shared our roll and looked out across the toy town, far down the valley to the dusty terraced foothills known as Red Mountain. The air was clear as window glass. We could see a prop plane landing in the pasture which served Aspen as its airstrip. It seemed to ride the currents which came as the bright sunlight burned away the morning fog.

82

Later, in the afternoon, people in leather harnesses with wings would go up the broad face of Ajax and, playing Icarus, throw themselves off the edge into the air, and float down, descending gently on the gusts of wind that came as warm and cool air changed places.

(Such humans with straps attached, soaring down the mountainside, great smooth flaps harnessed to their awkward bodies, must feel like grubs without their apparatus, like snails who have no shells. It would be like taking out your bones, to unhitch the gear that gave you shape and motion. In some way they were like the musicians: Aspen in those days abounded in vicarious anatomies.)

I didn't know exactly how human birds knew when and how to catch the currents. I wondered if physicists studied that. If Danny understood the mechanics of such stunts.

In high school I'd had a physics course, and we did the pulley and lever, and the screw and inclined plane. Our teacher was one of those men who had wanted to be someone famous and invent something famous, and who was instead teaching gifted children who didn't want to be famous and were tired of being inventive.

Besides, he taught us things we already knew and were weary of hearing about. My class had been hoisting and pulling and sliding things down and turning what screws we could since progressive nursery school. In kindergarten we'd constructed three-dimensional models that turned triangles into pyramids, circles into spheres, all that stuff, as we were, naturally, a pilot project of some National Science Foundation grant. And here was Mr. Hart, that was his name, setting up these labs with ropes and boards and stuff.

That may be why I never asked Danny about the air

currents: afraid he would give me the same stuff that any kid of five knows better than. In those days I could not bear to find him wrong in any way.

Yellow Dog chewed the last of the roll and laid her muzzle on my knee, and was glad for me. I poured some water from my canteen into my palm, and she lapped it and then licked my fingers.

She wasn't jealous of Danny; she'd called me Harry from the start.

Harry and Ebie

————————

W H E N I located Paducah—at the corner of the state which touches Illinois, Missouri, and Tennessee, not far from the great confluence of the Mississippi and the Ohio, itself at the juncture of the Tennessee with the Ohio—I was expecting a lesser Memphis, a sprawling river port.

It was, instead, a little backwater town, fortressed by hardwoods, secured by a levee. A town which maintained its Southeastern gentility and long past with a tincture of regret: if only we'd not been occupied by Union troops, if only Grandpa hadn't sold the mill.

No matter that the paper bustled with current worries —the country club's struggle to make a golf course on river bottom land once used for coon-dog kennels, the local unions' refusal to represent the twenty thousand migrants come to man the new plants—the core of the town's stable population shut itself in a small, unchanging world.

It seemed a fitting place for Danny and Ebie. They had moved to Paducah the year that the Tennessee Valley Authority built the country's largest coal-fired generator to power the Atomic Energy Commission's uranium plant, to which Danny drove his heavy head each day; but for all real purposes their lives were enclosed by the confines of their large, old, frame house.

In the heart of a once-fine neighborhood, it sagged in safety on a deep corner lot, insulated in the back by chestnuts, elm, and a boarded-up cistern, and in the front by fragrant rotting walnuts, unraked, rain-soaked leaves, and cracked cement sidewalks.

Inside high-ceilinged rooms, Danny and Ebie hoarded their stock of possessions: heavy oak pieces (sideboards, wardrobes, breakfronts), odd chairs, musty draperies, glass-front bookcases, threadbare orientals, and, in bathrooms with peeling paint and paper, a hoard of well-washed, mismatched towels. If they had money from Danny's work, little of it went for show.

We ate at the big round wood table in the kitchen, often with candles stuck in old spinning spools, always with cloth napkins from the sideboard. It was country; and it was nice. We had green-tomato pie and turnip cakes and banana fritters and sweet-potato turnovers, and little sugared tarts for dessert, things I'd never heard of but that tasted wonderful.

The only touch of grandeur was Ebie's piano. As Danny had said, there was a nine-foot Steinway in the living room —now piled with books and papers. I tried it: it was in tune and made a concert sound.

Since our meeting in Aspen, I'd done a quarter at Santa Cruz. Still not sure what I meant to do with myself, I'd taken, in preparation for this visit, a physics course.

We had, naturally, the pulley and lever, force and velocity, the amp and volt. Shades of Mr. Hart. I now knew how you could hang two weight-pans over a light ball-bearing pulley, using flexible cord, and, by adding another weight, produce changes in the velocity of the system. That and a few tricks with lever arms to get torque. None of which, needless to say, opened up avenues for me to talk to Danny. "How did your torque go today?" was not going to get me very far.

Not that I talked to him that much anyway, before the baby came. It bothered me, at first, that most of my time was spent with Ebie, although I saw it as a kind of favor to him, as he couldn't be there with her all day. Later, by the time she had the baby, I'd got caught up in the same protective attitude toward her that he had. She brought it out in you.

By the first of the year you could finally see that a baby was on the way. She had a low bulge, not under her rib cage where I somehow thought they protruded, but almost down between her thin hip bones.

We would go into the drafty living room with big cups of strong percolator coffee, which I had started drinking, and sit. At first this drove me crazy, as my usual habit is to move around a lot, but, gradually, I got used to it as she told me most of the facts about herself and her past.

"What did your mother die of?" I asked one morning. We were pursuing this morbid subject out of some tangential worry over the baby, and I remembered that she had lost her mother.

"She died of my papa, I guess." Ebie sat with her shoes off, and her feet, which were always freezing, tucked up under her.

"Would you care to explain—?"

"I'm not sure I can, Harry. You can't imagine that house in Cotton Valley if you haven't been there. They never left it. I mean, they never went out the door. I walked to school every day and then home. When I got to high school and wanted to date, and I would decide that I was going to a school party, it would be like walking in molasses. The boy would come, the ones who didn't know better, and Mama would be looking at the Sears catalogue and her pattern books, pretending she was wearing the dresses she saw, off in her dreamy world, and there would be nothing clean for me to put on, and Papa couldn't be interrupted to ask if I could go, and so the boy would go off, and I would stay in, and that would be that."

"Sounds awful." At such times I'd remember seeing her and Danny out the open door at the Epicure, and going up to them because they looked so normal, and I would have to smile at what I'd got myself into. Because the stories got worse as she got to know me better.

"They got their groceries delivered, which you could do then in towns like that in Louisiana—the Red Circle Grocer delivered them—and they never left the house, not ever. My papa sat in his back room all day long, locks on every door. And she stayed in, too. He'd got her against her will, and once he had, he kept her."

"How do you mean?"

"When he met her she was going with this other boy, she'd been going steady with him since sixth grade. And all that time, until she got engaged in twelfth grade, Papa had been after her, telephoning her, showing up at her house, following her. And she would tell him that she was not going with him, that she was going steady with this other boy, that she was going to get married. Well, the week of graduation, the week before the wedding, when she and the other boy were opening presents at her house, they got this sort of a black box, a painted wooden box that looked like a camera obscura, if you follow me, and it was addressed to her boyfriend, and the instructions said to look inside and wind it up and he'd see something. Well, he wasn't that dumb, so he pried off the slat at the top, and there was a sawed-off shotgun, fit into a painted dresser drawer, with a peephole cut in it, and a hand crank. That did it for the boyfriend, who gave up on fighting for Mama anymore, and just left town at that point."

"Did she tell you that?"

"No, she wouldn't. She never talked about such things. A nephew of my papa's told me. That was when I was very little; he, Armistead, was the only family outside of them I ever got to see."

"Jesus." The Roses Kennedy seemed pale by comparison.

"She gave up then, and married my papa. She didn't have the spirit to keep on. . . . I went back when she died, the first time since I ran away from home. There was all this filth; nobody had put the garbage out in months. She could of died of food poisoning, for that matter."

It became our habit that every day when we were in the two big stuffed chairs with the broken springs, facing the dark-draped windows and the littered piano, I could get her on the subject of her folks, for a brief time, before she got skittish and changed the subject.

(Other times, when I took her to the store, or went with her walking in the cold, because she felt she should exercise, we didn't talk about anything personal. Then I was there in the way a live-in nurse is, or a maiden aunt. Which in a sense was the function I served.)

I pieced together a weird gothic world, down there in

Cotton Valley. Her mother, Ledesma, couldn't bear to put anything away. Out of sight made her nervous. (Though you could make a case that this was a reasonable reaction to a gun in a box.) So apparently the place was a mess all the time, with her mother mooning over her catalogues, and things half out of dresser drawers, or in sacks on the kitchen floor, food left out that should have been put away, potato peelings rotting on the back porch, dirty clothes on the closet floor weeks past due for the washing machine.

It was all outside my ken, but fascinating in its way.

It seemed that her father, Cothron Brewster, barricaded himself inside a back bedroom where he kept all his belongings, and had an obsession that put my dad's hatred of Spain to shame. Her papa's entire life, at least in Ebie's memory, had been dedicated to tax evasion. Rather, to not paying taxes at all. Not his own, which were small pickings, but everyone's. That was his aim. He was head of a national organization which operated out of that house and claimed that wages were not in any way income, because income, as any fool knew, was earnings on capital, and wages, on the contrary, were payment for labor done, goods for services. Therefore it was unconstitutional and against the law to pay the government a percentage of any wages. He had apple crates filled with carbon copies of his letters to the membership and Internal Revenue, and card files of members' names. On the wall a framed plaque proclaimed: INCOME IS THAT WHICH COMES IN AS THE PRODUCE OF ONE'S BUSINESS, LANDS OR INVESTMENTS.

His workday consisted of organizing converts by mail. He claimed, Ebie said, to have got forty thousand members, and although he had a few helpers out in the field, he remained the national president, and all the confidential records were in his possession. His goal was a Supreme Court case overthrowing the taxation of wages.

As he peed in a slop jar, ate at his desk, and slept on a cot that blocked anyone from reaching his work, his nephew had to do the legwork of carrying stuff to the post office and bringing envelopes back, and even he, the nephew, had to come at a certain time of day, go to the back door, and say a password to get in.

"But when your mother died, what did your father do? Surely he went to the funeral?" I would ask these things which, before, it would never have occurred to me to ask, because I had learned that I could never second-guess the intrigue that had been Ebie's bread-and-butter past.

"Yes, he went to the cemetery. It was open casket and everybody came, curious to see her after such a time, and him because he'd been closeted so long. And I guess me also, as they would have known I was back. It was a big turnout. He cried his heart out and then went back to his old ways. Little towns get used to things like that."

She had taken to sitting with her arms wrapped around her middle. I would bring her coffee, and she'd let go with one hand to hold the cup, and then sometimes she'd switch arms. It wasn't clear if she was hurting or if that's what you did when you were pregnant.

I think the reason I was drawn to Ebie's stories of the past was because she existed in the world the way I did: apart from it. If my only friend had been a yellow dog, hers had been a kindly old grocer. We were two of a kind.

"How did you get out of there?" I asked her.

"How did I?" She gazed off. "That's not much of a

story, Harry. The end of my senior year in high school, when the summer was starting up, I asked could I get a job, and Papa said no, we didn't need the money, there was enough for me to do around there, keeping myself and my things straight, and they weren't going to let me be out on the streets selling, or in the stores where anybody could come in and take a fancy to me. I could see that the days at school were going to end and it would be like summer all the time; I'd be in there with them, stuck.

"So I ran away. If they had let me work at the drugstore, I'd probably be there still. What happened was, I simply did not come home from school the last day of class. I walked down the highway, scared to death that a patrol car or a teacher would see me and take me back, although I doubt, now, that anyone would have returned me. I might have got help from the whole town. Still, it's hard to say where loyalty is, in a case like that. They might have brought me home. Anyway, I had made up my mind to die if they did. . . . But nobody stopped me, and I walked all the way to Minden, and worked as a waitress until I got money to take a bus to Shreveport."

Every night I would plan, when we three were sitting around eating cornbread or fritters or blackberry cobbler, the questions that I was going to ask her the next morning.

One was, how did she hear about her mother's death, if she had never made contact with her folks after she ran away?

"When Danny and I moved here, to Paducah from Los Alamos, and I had the piano and my little girl, I wrote to my cousin Armistead, my daddy's nephew, where I was. For him not to tell, but that if anything had happened to them, or when it did, would he let me know. And so we wrote once in a while, and then when he went and found my papa crying all over the place and her dead on top of the bucket of potato peelings, he called."

"How did it feel to be back in that house again?"

She rocked herself with her arms. "I went to the funeral, and was going to spend the night with Papa, but I got scared, seeing him weeping and moaning out there in broad daylight. I got scared he'd take it in his head to keep me with him, especially now that he didn't have her. So I got in the car and headed home; but it got dark, and I was tired—I don't see well at night. I should have stopped. That's when we had the wreck, and Bea, who was with me, got sick." She paused. "I guess she was sick already."

"Were you hurt?"

"No. We had to take the bus, though, the car was ruined. It was a long trip, and the baby got dehydrated. I hadn't called Danny for fear it would drive him wild, so when we got home, she had this fever. We got her to the hospital, but it was too late."

She rocked. "I should have left her here with Danny. I had some idea that Bea should go back home with me to Cotton Valley while she was little, so she would have a vague memory of it and wouldn't need to go when she was older. Then she wouldn't have to ask me why I never took her. 'But you saw it,' I was going to say, 'when your grandma died. Remember?' Then if she ever went for herself, I was going to give her the address of a vacant lot. I was too ashamed of that place. But I was wrong to drag her down there with me. . . ."

By then I had decided that Danny's twisting on her hair and holding on to her sleeve all the time made a lot of sense. I could feel a similar tendency, quickly squashed, appear in myself. It all got to me, and although I'd vowed to quit smoking when I came to Paducah, by the end of a few weeks I'd dug out the pack I kept hidden in my socks.

Toward the last, I asked: "Did it hurt Danny a lot, losing your little girl?"

I had mixed feelings about that. On the one hand, I wanted him to be the kind of father who could never get over losing a kid. (I'd never known one, but you read about them.) On the other, it made me jealous in advance that he'd want to put on this new baby all the love he'd had for his first child.

"It's hard to tell," Ebie said, gazing off and holding tight. "She was part of the crowded world we had then. In Los Alamos, friends would be there, and the men would be shouting about some argument and get out the encyclopedia to settle it, or build models out of anything that was handy. They would use Bea's blocks and make out like they were explaining something to her, but they weren't. When she got to be about three she would hang around them and they would put on arguments that started out as explaining something to her, and end up back where they had always been, shouting at each other. Physicists do that a lot. She was happy, the way young children are, to watch the men argue. One time they decided to explain glaciers to her—she was almost four—and it was absurd. They got a block of ice from the ice house and set it on the floor, right down on the floor, on the bare boards, and they slid *Brittanica*s down it and hollered at each other about moraines, until the ice half melted. Bea didn't understand anything; finally she squatted in the puddle and wet the floor. They never noticed.

"Another time it was the solar system. She'd just turned

94

four, I know because it was the week before we went back to Cotton Valley. . . . Danny and an old friend were going to show her the heavens. They had this orange and grape-fruit and lemon in the air, waving them around, and explaining orbits and eclipses. For years after, though we don't do that anymore, I used to say: 'Look, Danny, the lemon has risen.' "

She clasped her middle with both arms, and I picked up her empty cup off the floor. She looked wet in the eyes, but generally tight and dry in the face. She was very big all of a sudden, and she had got very slow. She wore her hair tied off her cheeks with a ribbon, which looked strange on a woman who'd recently turned forty-one.

"That all stopped when we lost Bea." She drank the hot coffee I brought. "In that way you could say he missed her. He missed how it used to be."

"Is that when you stopped playing the piano?"

"Is it?" She looked far away. "I guess. There was no longer need to. I had started in self-defense. They shouted all the time. In New Mexico and then here, argued all the time. I couldn't get used to it, ever. I had to balance it, to take my turn; so Danny gave me lessons, and the piano. Then when it got too much I would play, and he would say to them, 'Shut up, she's playing,' and they would. But then there was no need. It was quiet all the time."

She mostly wore big-sized men's flannel shirts now, and, over that, a dark green man's cardigan, heavily ribbed. That was inside the drafty house. When we went out, she put on a poncho that she had got in the West, which looked more or less like a horse blanket. All that seemed awkward, the amount of clothes needed to cover that one small bulge.

It wasn't all that cold, but the chill and light snow reminded me of Aspen, and I would wear my hiking boots and Woolrich jacket when we went out, and find myself missing the Epicure and my hikes up Ute Trail.

The question I finally worked up to ask was: how come she was having this baby?

It's unbelievably stupid, my thinking then; but I was under the assumption that after a number of years of not doing it, Ebie and Danny had decided, for some reason, to have intercourse in order to make this child.

That's where I was coming from. You don't know what you don't know. There didn't seem to me at that time to be any correlation between sex, which was something you did alone, and sharing a bed, which, like all sharing, had to do with class.

Ebie had mentioned that she had slept with her mother (poor, same sex) and Danny with his brother (poor, same sex); so I attributed the fact that they shared a bed in this old house with four bedrooms and three baths, all half furnished, to their having got used to it when they were little. In fact, as the bedroom I was using was downstairs, they didn't even have to share a floor, but I thought that had never occurred to them.

So when I finally asked, "How come you decided to have another baby after so long?" it must have sounded unusually dumb to her, even for Harrod Roncevaux.

"What?" she asked.

That was what she said when I was not getting through; it was a helpful cue, that "What?"

"Why didn't you have one before, after you lost Bea?" That was a more positive way of putting it.

She looked vague. "Oh, I don't know, Harry. I just left it out. I don't know why I did. I didn't forget; I just left it out."

"Hmmmmm." I didn't know what *it* was, or where it got omitted from. My ears felt hot. Here I thought it was what you put in that did it, not what you left out. So much for progressive sex education.

"On one level," she went on, musing aloud, "I must of decided he wanted another. And that it had to be now or never, me being forty. That's all I can figure."

One thing was clear anyway, and maybe that was what I had really wanted to know: Danny hadn't been in on it. Except that I knew from biology that he had to have been. So actually nothing was clear. Except that she considered it her doing.

"Are you sorry?"

She was sitting on the stiff horsehair couch. "I don't know." She switched her hugging and drinking arms.

"But I guess when it's on the way, then you want it, don't you?" (No doubt I was doing this dumb fishing around because I longed to get a resounding "yes" to that question.)

"I don't know," she said. "I'm not sure."

I got us another cup and unplugged the pot. I had run out of things to ask. The baby had better go ahead and come. It was the middle of February already and two weeks late, and I had run out of things to wonder.

"You were good to come stay with us," Ebie said. She was sort of rocking back and forth, holding her middle fiercely. "I was at my wits' end."

"Glad to do it. I was going to take the quarter off anyway." Which wasn't completely true, nor wholly false.

"I thought it would be here the end of January, you know."

"I needed to get away a while."

97

"I didn't know who to get. Danny can't stay alone; he can't stay a night by himself. It has to do with his daddy, his being afraid that he'll end up helpless like that if he's left alone. At any rate, I could hardly have put an ad in the paper, and all our friends have scattered. We will, too, I suppose, next year; no need to stay on here, with the trips to West Virginia out of the way." She looked worn out. "Besides, Danny liked you right away." She smiled at me.

"This is a pretty place," I said. "Paducah."

"But you will get back in school?"

"Have to, if my folks are going to pay my way."

"They only give you money if you're in college?"

"Yeah."

"Not much incentive to get out."

"That's what I said."

"It would make more sense if they paid you only if you had a job." She laughed.

I laughed, too. Because I had already thought of that. "I asked them that—when I was young, I mean. I said if what they wanted me to do was work, then why not pay me to make money?"

She looked at me, pleased by the whole idea. At the idea of parents anywhere thinking like that. We laughed again, and it was one of the few times we saw something the same way, and that felt good. I liked her a lot at that moment: because she could come up with something like that, which showed she was able to get past herself.

"What did they say?"

"My mother said: 'That would be two incomes for the same work.' My father said: 'You've already got more than nine-tenths of the world, what do you want?'"

She liked that. She gazed off a while and then she told

me, in a tone that said this was a secret, that she'd once asked her mother if she could take some money to school.

"What for?"

"That's what she said, so I made up some story. The truth was I couldn't stand never having money. She packed my lunch, so there was no lunch money. I could have saved that. She would look in the lunch sack when I got home to see what did I eat, every day."

"So what did you want the money for?"

"To *have*." She got up then, unfolded her legs and put her feet back in her lace-up shoes, and went into the kitchen. She brought back the mason jar that she used for a flour canister. While I watched, she dug around in it and brought out a little marble bag, made of printed cotton, covered with flour. She undid the drawstring and showed me sixty cents, two quarters and a dime. "I never spent it. I took it with me to Shreveport and then out West and then here. I left it behind when I went down home to bury Mama—maybe that was bad luck."

"You were afraid she'd take it back." I felt I could say that to her now.

"You're right." She smiled. "And maybe she would have. It makes me mad that I still have it; I still have nearly everything I ever got. It reminds me of Papa and makes me sick at myself, hoarding. I don't tell Danny."

"My trouble is losing things."

"That is the danger, isn't it?"

"Yeah."

We didn't talk for a while. I could see she was putting away the morning, getting ready to take our walk or go to the store.

Then she said: "Maybe that's what I wanted, to give

Danny someone else." She returned the marble bag to the flour jar. "What good luck it was, running into you in Colorado."

"It's more like I ran into you."

"We need to get the groceries now. Before it comes."

Ebie

I had arrived in Paducah the week after Christmas. I could have come on Christmas Day, but I didn't want to admit that to Danny and Ebie. The holidays at home had been: thin. My folks seemed surprised to see me there. The commercialism of my appearance suggested that they should take their minds from the really needy. I got the offer of money or a trip to Mexico City. As I did not want to see the poor in Mexico any more than I wanted to hear about them at home, I took a check instead.

Christmas dinner I ate out at a motel restaurant alone. Dad spent the day writing Euzkara in his journal; Mom spent it sending letters off around the state to see what causes were in need of advocacy. It was a cold day in a warm climate, and I was really glad to leave.

In Paducah, as is clear, I wasn't doing much to help either Danny or Ebie, but at least they had asked me there, and fed and watered me, and walked me, and talked to me.

I don't want to leave Ebie for good, like that, seen through the filter of young, dumb Harrod Roncevaux. So before we get to Danny, who is, after all, the reason I got into this and stayed to the end, and the girl, I want to let Ebie tell her own story.

Later, when she was dead and I was grown, I pieced together most of what I hadn't known. So I'll improvise from that.

However, it isn't easy to give you a woman who can save sixty cents for twenty-five years—and give a baby away in half an hour.

She knew she had to go home. Ever since Bea died she had felt the glue slip away that held her here with Danny. Maybe making another one had been a frantic attempt to attach herself once and for all, but it hadn't worked.

Her cousin Armistead wrote: her papa lived in his own filth because he would not go out or let anyone in; he thought they should put her papa away, as he was too senile to stay on in that house with its climbing glories and crumbling, boarded-up outhouse. Armistead's wife was dead.

Had she known that someone would come along to help out Danny, she would never have tried another baby. She could foresee now that if she hadn't done this, Danny, with his old daddy dead, going crazy with nothing to fill the gap, would make do with the boy. She could have left them a hot supper and gone, if she had known.

She was all set to run away, straight from the hospital. She'd put the marble bag with its sixty cents among her things, the same as she had done before when she had left at seventeen.

"It's time, Danny," she called to the men, who still sat at the kitchen table. She had gone off to pack, letting them think she'd gone to count the pains. She had no need of that. She knew when it was ready, you always knew: when it felt like the metal stave on a barrel pulled to breaking.

In the car she reminded Danny, "Don't stay with me,

now. I want to have it alone. You promised. In case I'm too old, in case it's not all right. It will take the night. I'll have them call you when it's over. You promised."

Danny had hesitated, but the boy was there. He did not have to face an empty house. That was why she had brought Harry there, not to drive her to the store or sit marking time over coffee but to take her place.

At the hospital she registered as Elizabeth Brewster, unmarried. Her ring was in the marble bag. The doctor, who knew her only by that name, was an old country man and did not know the newcomers. He was competent; delivering babies was a lifetime's familiar habit. She had told him that she was divorced and that the father might come roaring around, trying to break down doors, claiming them still married. He was to say Miss Brewster was quarantined.

She'd prepared Danny, hadn't she, that he wasn't going to have the baby, always mentioning her age, that something could go wrong, not to count on another? She had told him about the freak in Cotton Valley who lived in a baby buggy on the front porch of the house with the sweet gum for twenty-seven years and never grew, except his head. She made out she had seen the big-headed baby, though she had only heard of it.

It gave her guilt that she had got pregnant without asking Danny. Although she hadn't lied; she reminded herself of that. Every night of the world when he rolled her on her side and began to do it, he asked: "Do you have it in?" Every night of the world. It had been that way since Bea died and Ebie hadn't wanted to do it anymore, afraid of getting pregnant. "Do you have it in?" She could shut her eyes and hear that, until the asking became a way of saying that he wanted it. "Do you have it in?" and her gown was up and he was in her.

That night he hadn't asked. In his head he must have, the way he always did, but not out loud. She would have said no. And then it would have been for him to decide. Would he have told her, "Go get it"? Or would he have said, "Then leave it out"? She had wanted that, for him to decide. But it hadn't worked that way, and she hadn't spoken, and, a few weeks later, in Colorado, she'd told him she was sure that she was going to have a baby. He'd never asked her how come, or when. He'd been overjoyed, like a great bear at a jar of honey. It had shamed her, how much he wanted it.

She had been eleven when she first began to fantasize about Armistead. He was twice her age at that time, which made him seem settled, although he was still a young man. It had been natural; he was her only link with the world outside.

Once they had had a fountain drink together in the drugstore, in plain sight of everyone—and she had lived on that for years. How it had happened was that the grocer at Red Circle Grocer had taken a liking to her and felt sorry for her. And when he judged her old enough, he'd said to her mama on the phone: "Ledesma, I don't mind charging and delivering for you, but you got that kid what could pick things out a lot more careful than I can. Why don't you send her up? I don't mind saying I'm right busy and don't always pick out the very best goods. I'll keep an eye on her." Then the grocer, a bent old white-haired man with a cough (that he died of), would have the sacks all filled when she got there, and she could go have a Coke float or

an "800"—a chocolate milk on ice that was her favorite—
with some of the kids from school, and he would add the
quarter he gave her onto the grocery bill.

One time when she was there, hanging out a minute
where all the kids went, Armistead came in, and he did a
big double-take on seeing her out of the house on Elm, and
he invited her to sit at the fountain counter with him, and
everyone saw that. From that time on she pretended to
herself that he would have married her but for the fact that
they were cousins and everyone knew that cousins made
monsters when they married.

All the girls at school had heard the same things: that
cousins made monsters; that cousins could marry anyway
in Arkansas; that you could get married in Oklahoma at
twelve without consent; that anybody could get a divorce
in Reno, Nevada, with no questions asked. They all knew
those things.

But Ebie also knew that Armistead would never shame
himself that way, or leave his daddy's store. Still, imagining it gave her something to live on.

"Why don't you get yourself pregnant, little honey,"
the grocer would say, "and leave them crackpots?" And
she'd smile and collect the sacks and get ready to ride with
him to deliver them.

She knew he wouldn't be as kind if he knew what she was
thinking.

But by the time she was seventeen, she was tired of pretending. Armistead was twenty-eight and looking to get
married. It was time for her to go. She began storing stuff:
the fifty cents her mother gave her to carry in her shoe in
case she started her period at school and needed to get something out of the machine, the dime Armistead had given

her the time they'd met in the drugstore. Slowly she carried things off. She stuck her pink sweater in her lunch sack and put her sandwich and cookie in her panties under her skirt. It was May and hot, with flies and gnats and steamy vines; no one, not even Mama, would think to look to see if a sweater was missing. She took her loafers the same way, when she had her sandals on. And her hair barrettes, and her one good nightgown.

Then, the last day of school, she left. The way she told Harry. (Most of what she told him had been true; or true enough to keep him from asking any more.) It wasn't true that she and her mama slept in the featherbed together. She had slept between her mama and papa until she was big, maybe eight, and then, when she got too big for that, she'd moved into the little room where her mama kept her sewing and mail-order catalogues, and her mama had moved in with her. And her papa moved to his cot.

Her papa slept like a log and when he rolled over against you he snored. Her mama slept like a feather and half the night she scratched herself almost raw; and every morning when she got up she'd go look at her tongue in the bathroom mirror over the sink and say: "It's coated." Something about her mama's skin and mouth were always driving her crazy.

Her mama had a famous family. Whenever her papa was out of earshot, which was all the time in later years, since he never left his room, that's what her mama talked about. How they had once been famous. Her mama had framed and hung on the wall the letter her great-granddaddy had written to his bride before their wedding. In curly handwriting and faded ink, her mama's granddaddy, Righteous Devoe, proclaimed:

It is and must be the natural sequence of human life that as we together with our bright and happy ideals of life approach the brightness and sunshine of our marriage, we join together the north and the south, the temperate and the tropical zones, the aged and the young. Rest easy my love that not one single stain, blemish or scar will rest on the ancestry of your children. Yours will have in their veins the blood that has made America what it is today, the blood of the men and women who braved the hardships of the new world for conscience sake, who filled the south, but notably our great state of Louisiana, with bold hearts and stalwart aims. Please know that you are now a part of this writer's devotion to home and country, and all that is brightest and best in American life.

Your devoted,
R.

Her mama would read that every day, and then she would look at her pattern books and mail-order catalogues, and then Ebie would come home from school. And that was her world.

Armistead had told her about himself, the time they had the sodas together. That at his house on Sunday when he was little the men would take off their Sunday shirts after dinner and sit out front in their undershirts and suspenders and talk about when they were boys; and the women would go back to the bedroom and take off their Sunday dresses and hang them up and lie on the beds in their slips with the fan on and some iced tea and talk about when they were girls. And the little kids, who weren't either one yet, would go back and forth, inventing skinned knees or abuses or thirst, from one group to the other to see how it was out front and in the back.

And Ebie had wanted to be with those ladies more than anything in the world. Whenever she was tired, she thought of it. She'd imagine that she would take off her silk Sunday dress and lie on the chenille bedspread in a clean, pin-neat house, and listen to the men, Armistead and his friends, in their undershirts on the porch, talking and smoking on a Sunday afternoon.

She went back to her mama's funeral with little Bea. That was because she forgot how it was in Cotton Valley: that you might not get away. The real reason, which she hadn't told Harry, was that she'd wanted Armistead to see her baby, who was four then, and so pretty; she'd been so proud. Bea was a namesake for the famous granddaddy the same as Ebie, whose real name was Elizabeth Righteous Brewster. But in school her name was too long to write out, so she signed herself E.B., so even the teachers started calling her Ebie. The baby was B. Righteous Wister, and that was nice, and they called her Bea.

But Armistead, who was forty then, didn't seem to recall what Ebie had meant to him in that other time. He was standing in his good suit with a wife on his arm—a wife who got to lie on Sundays with the ladies in their slips before the fan while the men sat out front in their undershirts.

Ebie had touched the climbing glories on the shabby house, seen that the decrepit outhouse was still standing, and left town. Even then she could tell that little Bea was flushed, that her mouth was cracked and peeling from the fever. Her papa wanted her to stay, but she'd been too scared even to get the baby to a doctor.

Danny had been looking for someone to take care of when she met him in New Mexico. His mother was dead, and his daddy was way back in West Virginia. It was never going to work out with the nurse he lived with, Louise, because she was off on her shift all the time, and when she got home she only wanted to talk about what bad things she'd seen, and those very bad things were what Danny wished he was looking after for somebody.

Ebie was that somebody. Danny wanted to teach her everything that he knew. The shouting and the mess on the living-room floor, the block of ice, the orange and grapefruit, that was all for her. "Jesus, what did they teach you down there in the swamps of Louisiana?" Then he would demonstrate the solar system, or the glacial gouging. One day there was an eclipse, and Danny took a shirt cardboard and put a pinhole in it, and she watched the miracle of the tiny disc with a piece nibbled out of it appear on the sheet of paper in her hand below the cardboard. Nights they were alone with no one around to join in the shouting, he would read to her aloud.

Finally Louise moved on, and Ebie and Danny got married.

Danny saw that she liked music, so he had her take lessons from a woman whose husband was also out there being a physicist in the mountains. Ebie discovered that the piano was different when the house was cold or when it was warm, and Danny rewarded her for noticing by buying her a grand of her own.

He wanted her to go to school. He had come from people that didn't have schooling, and he wanted to convey to her what a difference it made when you understood things instead of just lived with them. But she had never made sense of school, and had a fear of getting herself back inside any place like that, where you had to be, and couldn't leave when you wanted, and had to tell them why if you missed. So they compromised. He didn't really want anyone else handling her education anyway: that would have been like letting his old daddy be taken care of in a hospital.

So he set out a program, and she read a book a week for him, with two weeks off for vacation. She did it still; it was habit. Last week she'd read *Les Misérables* by Victor Hugo. Her books stood in special cases by themselves, so that in eighteen years she should have had nine hundred books, but they weren't all there, because she used the library mostly in the early days, because libraries had most of the classics you couldn't always buy.

She had got in the habit over the years of tackling her book the first thing Monday morning and reading on it until she was through. And then practicing the piano as hard as she could, until Thursday at supper. Then, if she had not picked out too thick a book, or too many hard pieces, she was through, and could spend three days doing nothing, not learning anything, or working at anything, just sitting around in her pin-neat house in her slip.

Armistead's wife died of cancer; he was fifty-one. He wrote her the day after it happened, in a circumspect letter mostly about the fact that her papa was so senile that he hardly knew what he gave Armistead to mail to the membership or what came in from around the country, most of it postage due, which came out of Armistead's pocket. They should put him in a home, he wrote. If she came down, he'd assist her to do that.

That was the night she left the diaphragm out. She didn't know, even in herself, whether it was to take a baby back to Armistead or to make one that would force her to stay with Danny. She didn't think it would do any good to know, not at this point.

Labor was long, stretching her back like spinal meningitis and stringing her teeth like beads. A final tightrope it took five hours to snap.

It was a girl. The nurse said that was good; that girls were easier to place. Fathers didn't like their names to be carried on by someone that wasn't their blood. And born on Valentine's to boot—they put a pink bow on the baby's crib.

Ebie, drained and lying flat and wiped out on the pillow, wanted to say that her baby had the blood in her veins that made America famous, but she didn't. She looked away. She wished it hadn't been a girl, because Danny would want that so, to make up for Bea. If it had been a boy she could have thought he had one already, back at home, and grown at that. But then, if it had been a boy, she might have hated that he wasn't going to get to name it for his daddy. . . .

She slept briefly until she was steady again and then got up and got dressed. When you placed a baby they let you hold it once, to see it was all right, and to be sure you knew what you were doing, and then they didn't bring it to you again. The other mothers fed theirs and got attached, but you didn't. They let you have that one time, and if you were sure, then you signed the papers giving it away. Her doctor had somebody waiting; he had worked it out. Good people. It wasn't going to a home. If it went through a home, you didn't know who got it; besides, that meant that many more hands passing it on.

The doctor was old, bald, and liked babies. That was enough for Ebie.

"*Be Righteous*," she whispered to the bloody, bawling little thing. Then she shut her eyes as they took it away.

She slipped out of the hospital in her robe pulled over her dress, her robe hiked up, her coat over that, out the side door, down the service stairs. She was always running away. The marble bag was in her purse. She dragged her suitcase behind her.

We were still up. Danny was listening to me play a Schubert sonata on my violin when she came in.

She hadn't known she wouldn't feel like staying at the hospital, couldn't stay, and so would have to come back here. She hadn't thought how it would be.

"Ebie!" Danny leaped to his feet. "How did you get here? At this hour?"

"Walked."

"What happened?" He was frantic, imagining all the worst things that could have brought her back this time of night, her robe spilling down below her coat. "Did it die?"

"No. It's all right." She tried to focus on his face.

"You shouldn't have walked. Jesus, where were the lunatics who're supposed to be looking after you?" He rushed to lift her, started with her to the couch. "Hush," he was saying even as he shouted questions at her. "Was it all right? When did it come?" His big misshapen hands held her as if he couldn't decide whether to cradle her or shake her.

"She's bleeding," I told him, seeing a deep stain on the rug where she'd been standing.

"I gave her away," she said.

"What?" He snapped her shoulders. "You what?"

I wanted to cry.

Ebie looked as if terror had seized her by the neck, whipped her like a dog with a rabbit. What if we turned all the feeling on her we'd been saving for the baby? What if she was kept in a buggy on the porch for twenty-seven years? Or left to rot away like a bucket of potato peelings? She had done all this and yet here she was, had gained nothing by it, would never get home.

She hadn't known she'd faint when she told him, but she did.

Harry and Danny

I went berserk. Hollered at Danny about his legal rights. Made a trip to the courthouse; called up a Legal Aid clinic. Made a trip to the hospital to look at birth records, which, naturally, as I had no claim, they weren't about to show me. It may be they thought I was a nut trying to make trouble for Ebie, who was in there again and in bad shape.

They might have been right.

She had lost a lot of blood and got an infection, and so had to go back; she was fairly hysterical at the idea, but they put her on a different floor.

Danny said to let the matter drop. It drove me nuts, and for days I threatened, and argued, and pleaded. But whereas he, the father, had rights, I, a no-kin, sometime college student, had none. So I let it go. Contenting myself with a lifetime burden of guilt that I had come to help Danny, and had failed totally in the one thing which counted for something: getting him his baby back.

I used to think about the kid a lot, for no special reason. Wonder how it would be to wake up in some calm place with a pink bow on your bassinet, all that, and never know that you came from Ebie bleeding all over the rug, and

Danny pounding the table with his fist, and the music blaring all the time.

Things were different with Ebie not there. Danny came home and the first thing he poured himself a milk glass full of whiskey and the second he put on a whole opera. Wagner or, if he'd done that two days in a row, Verdi, and he would turn it up so loud that the bass vibrated the lamps and the treble became a screeching wobbly line. We'd sit in the middle of the shrieking, bellowing, wailing voices for a couple of hours, then he'd turn it off for a spell. Even if he put on one of his old shellacs to let me hear Alma Gluck singing with Efrem Zimbalist on violin for the old Victor Talking Machine Company, his real treasures, he had it so loud the record scratches sounded like a second accompanist.

One night, after they'd hammered the stones on Aïda's head, I felt the way I used to when I played violin all the time, that I was the wood vibrating. My head seemed to be the speaker amplifying the sound: Harrod, human woofer and tweeter. It took a while before I quit shaking bits of sound loose from my ears in the vast living room. I said: "It takes ten minutes for the silence to catch up."

"Too loud? Why didn't you say? Ebie complains sometimes. I guess I need the volume to get it through this thick head of mine. Ebie is a lover of music—" He always got a mad, hurt look when he talked about her. "I can hear fine when she plays; somebody live is better any time than anybody canned. Besides, nobody plays the way she does." Which pain and anger sent him into the kitchen for another glass of whiskey.

"You're fond of music yourself," I said, loosening my ears with my finger.

"I used to play," he said, getting off the subject of Ebie, "when I was a little kid. Did you know that, Harry? My mother played by ear, and we had this old upright on which she taught me how to make chords. Every time my daddy caught us at it, me sitting up there by her, he'd give her hell. It was the only time I recall him letting go his temper. He thought she was making a sissy out of me. He'd bent his back working, so he wanted his boys to amount to something."

"It was different at my house," I said. "Being a musician was better than a lot of stuff."

"Well, a fiddler's not the same. My old daddy played the fiddle, though he considered that somewhat the same as whittling, something to do when you couldn't go out. Anyway, his preoccupation for me and my brother was job. He wanted us to have a first-class job. He'd report, 'Your uncle's got hisself a good paying position in retail. Been to Honolulu and Washington, D.C., they have.' He'd tell me about the cousin who got into insurance or trucks or whatever was the coming field. 'Trains is a thing of the past,' he'd announce. 'Trucks is the coming wave of the future.' Or implements, or camper trucks, or computers. To the last, that's what he had it in his head I did, and it pleased him. 'Computers is the future,' he'd tell anyone who'd listen."

Talking about his daddy, he was getting relaxed again.

"What happened to my playing chords," he went on, "was that one time I got caught with my hands under the sweater of Threkeld's girl, who was willing enough, but I should have known better. Anyhow, he and a buddy took me out and jumped around on my hands for a while on the gravel pile behind the school. My old daddy tried not to cheer up at that, but it was no secret he felt that I had it coming for making music—even though at that time I was half grown and playing football.

"I'd have let them kill me before I'd have told my daddy what I'd been doing with Threkeld's girl. He would have disowned me, more than likely. He had no vices and he thought that was the way you were put on this earth to live. The highest bit of praise he knew to give was: 'He's got no habits.' " Danny threw back his head and laughed. "That was the highest. What it meant was you didn't drink or chase or gamble or chew. I grew up thinking I'd got all the habits there was."

At times like that I would study him—the uranium-heavy head, the ancient tweed suits, the burr hair and whiskey face, the stubby legs hardly long enough to serve a good end-table—and I would long to look like Danny.

(I had this horror of ending up like my folks. The Roses K., Wendell and Marie, looked like wizened eight-year-olds at fifty. Yet pictures I'd seen of them when they were small showed them looking like little puckered grandparents in diapers. They'd be aged kids all their days. It was no recommendation for a life without habits.)

"I guess you hated to lose your father," I said.

He nodded. "He went on Easter Sunday. I knew he wasn't long, but it hurts you when they finally go, no matter how prepared you are. I went up there every week at the last. He needed me to carry him out in the sun. He wasn't a man who was comfortable indoors. When I'd come home, at the last, I'd fix him something to eat, so the lady down the street could take off, and we'd mostly talk.

We'd go down the list of his friends not underground yet, those with habits and those without. He kept up with everyone he'd ever been to school with or worked with or even traded with. He'd have a bad word to say for those who stayed in railroads when trucks came in, or dry goods when they should have got into fast foods."

"It must have meant a lot to him, having you come around."

But he had clouded up. He'd touched something deeper than what he was saying. His words had stirred up something that overflowed in a burst. "He appreciated it, that's right. They have to appreciate it or there's no point. Take those Grade A lunatics in the swamp, that's a wasted effort." He drained his glass. "I was barely back from looking after my daddy when she got home with the baby sick. I should have gone with her; but I couldn't trust myself not to cripple that lunatic. Actually, do you know, Harry, I never laid eyes on that man. Married to his daughter for more than twenty years and never set eyes on him. We got married and he never once—" He looked the way he had when Ebie walked home in her robe, torn between wanting to cry and wanting to break something. "That baby," he said. "I miss her every day of my life. I miss her little face and her voice saying 'Daddy' the way she did. She was the smartest little thing you ever saw." He got tears in his eyes that rolled down his splotched red cheeks.

After a while I asked him did he feel a lot of guilt about the atom bomb.

"How's that?" He blinked his eyes.

I was angry: here he was, crying like that in the middle

of the living room over a kid long dead, when he wouldn't let me even try to find the one that Ebie gave away.

"The A-bomb," I said. Not caring that he must only have been in college when it was dropped. Forgetting that Danny was Danny and would not be insulted.

He cleared his mind with a fresh glass of whiskey, and immediately started talking to me about physics—as if I'd meant it.

"I was just a kid then, Harry. It didn't seem germane, splitting the atom. Not that I didn't share a lot of worry later when we were messing with the H-bomb; but that's old stuff, blowing things up. The problem now is to contain it. We've been hovering on the brink of controlling fusion for ten years and we're no further along. They work on getting the temperature up there and increasing the pressure, but it can't be done the way they're doing it. They're trying too hard is the point. You know, physicists today are in the same league with the bunch that came before Galileo. They ran around asking themselves: 'What does it take to make something move?' Then they'd decide you had to have something to push an object or something to pull it. Then Galileo comes along and says: 'Forget looking and *think*.' He asks them: 'What would happen to a wheel if the road was smooth as glass, would it ever stop rolling?' He tells them: 'It isn't the pushing or pulling, it's something else that makes things stop and go.' He tells them: 'Figure out what if you removed it would make things roll forever, and you have the cause.' Physicists today don't get the message. They're working too hard: trying to bash a couple of atoms together with magnetic force or laser beam, working for the temperature and pressure of the sun's interior. . . . They don't *think*. This glass of whiskey has enough energy to last the planet's lifetime, and they don't ask what it is that *keeps* these atoms from fusing all over the place all the time, and hunt for that."

He had brightened up a lot, being on this subject, and talked on and on until I was even glad when he looked up and asked, "How about a little music?"

It never occurred to me then that he talked about his job so little because the loss of what he wanted to be working on out in New Mexico cut closer to home for him than even his old daddy or his little girl.

At least my distracting him on that occasion had one side effect: whenever we were taking a break from the deafening sound, and time began to drag for him, he would go back to physics.

"Let me tell you how I happened into the field, Harry. It was self-defense, the way you get into most things. After I'd tried to get my geometry teacher to see a shorter way to work a theorem and she sent me to the principal, and I'd told my trig teacher a better way to work a problem and she'd hurled an eraser at me, my advisor said I better get myself an academic scholarship to college somewhere, or else I was going to get myself expelled.

"So I thought back to what had I been interested in and recalled a unit we had in geography in eighth grade. I remember getting mad at noticing that if the ground under your feet had quit making itself in the coal era, then you were a poor boy; but if the earth you were walking on had turned itself into pockets of oil, then you were going to be a rich boy. I mean, out in Texas your sharecropper uncle can hit oil on his back forty and he's chairman of the board and his daughters all marry dentists, whereas back where I came from, the best thing you could hit in your backyard was your wife. And clear as a bell it came to me that the whole ballgame had been decided millions of years before we were born.

"Well, being a smart kid, the way you are in school, I reasoned that if nature could figure out how to turn swamps into whatever she wanted, then why couldn't we? And we will. You'll live to see, Harry, nice, clean, sweet-smelling gasified coal and, one day, sunshine gas pumping along in the very pipelines we're using now. And that's how it came about that I got into research in the first place."

"I'm still waiting for inspiration to hit me, I guess," I said. The truth was his talk of work threatened me more than most things. The Roses K. had made plain that you had to start with a Cause, which I didn't have; and Danny's variation, that you started with a Vision, didn't help much either. Secretly, I thought it a shame that working for money had fallen into disfavor.

"You're not planning to stay with the fiddle, are you?"

And I had to smile at that, as he'd said it in the same way his old man must have objected to him playing the piano. "No, I guess not."

"So what do you like to do with yourself?"

What I liked mostly was to move around. I'd been walled up in the drafty living room of this old house for weeks, and it was getting to me. I'd imagined before I came that Danny and I would have a ritual the same as Yellow Dog and I had; that we'd walk around the block and name the trees, or at least trudge in step as we reminisced.

"I like the outdoors," I said.

"Not me. I can't take much of it at a time. The trouble

is I can't enjoy a walk through a cornfield without a pencil and tape-measure. You have to have a different kind of curiosity to be interested in nature. My daddy had that. He could sit out any time of day or night. He learned the stars when he worked the day shift; and the weather, high and low for every day of the year, when he worked the night shift. He could tell you to the hour when we'd get the first frost."

"I'd like to work outside, I think." And at the moment, anyway, it was true. Worn out with worrying over this pair and their losses, I wanted nothing more at that moment than to catalogue all the berries in the south of Alabama or list the fir trees in the Klondike.

"Well, a naturalist is not a bad occupation."

Naturalist. That had appeal. (Besides, I couldn't think of a single thing in the whole world that my folks would understand less. Even violinists were acceptable. But some guy who went around saying, "Hello, birds. Hello, trees"? Jesus. What could be worse for Liberals than a life's work whose aim was to leave everything the way you found it?)

Cheered up by the idea, that night I tried my first glass of whiskey as we put on an old shellac of Caruso.

The next morning Ebie came home, recovered from her infection, if not her depression.

"My daddy's got a dog locked in there with him," she said out of the blue. We sat in the living room, the three of us, like a family, after eating a stew that Danny had made. He still did the cooking, although she said she'd be up to it in a day or two.

"How do you know that?" Danny sat close by her on the stiff couch, fingering her long hair, which now hung straight to her shoulders.

"I think I dreamed it; but the nurse said that Papa's nephew called. He may have told me."

"Might do that lunatic good to have some company for a change, even a dog."

"He won't let it out." Ebie looked frantic.

"Maybe he mistakes it for your mama." Danny laughed, but checked himself to be sure that Ebie wasn't going to take offense.

"Maybe it's Mama, come back in dog form." She made a joke, too, but shakily.

I was shut out, the way I'd been in Aspen, but now it felt more the way you imagine it should be when you're a kid: that the grown-ups will talk about things you don't understand, but with you there. Talk about secrets which you'll grow into knowing in time. For the moment—a childhood moment—you can imagine your grandmother, say, turned into a sweet old yellow dog in a new incarnation. It can be literal in your mind even though you know they don't mean it that way. Metaphors. That's how you imagine grown-ups to talk, close together, holding on, with a fire in the grate to shut out the wind.

"Play a little, Harry," Ebie asked me. "Did you play while I was in that awful place?"

"Some nights." She and I exchanged a look, or I felt we did, that said we both knew most of the music around here was Danny's booming operas.

"It's my turn, then." She pulled her green housecoat up like a petticoat and marched over to the grand piano.

Danny looked as if the lights had just come on in a dark house.

She played the first swift section of Debussy's Sonata in G Minor. Then, without turning around, she moved into Mozart's Concerto in D Minor.

"Did you hear that?" Danny asked. "Didn't I tell you?"

He was right. Doing what I always said musicians did, she came alive when she touched the keys, becoming only a set of hands that pulled the sound from the great harp strings under the curving wood. I wanted to break my violin on the spot. I had been making practice; she made music. No wonder Danny had been deaf without it.

The Mozart walked and then danced as it gathered speed, all around the room until it was everywhere and you could not tell where it originated. After she ended, a few notes clung to the walls and furniture, the way soap bubbles do, and you were afraid to breathe too hard for fear of bursting them.

I thought I ought to leave. It seemed useless to stay, now that Danny had back what he had missed so long.

He went over and put his hands on her cheeks, pulling her face against his chest as she sat on the piano bench. He turned around to me, beaming all over. "Didn't I tell you? Did you hear that? She used to play for me every night."

She was talking to him. "In the hospital I got to thinking that you wanted the new baby in part so I'd play again. At least, I thought, I could do that. I got scared, Danny, when I was carrying the baby, afraid it was a jinx. But now it's like at the beginning, to play again."

"Should I leave?" I asked, my voice cracking.

She smiled. "No, Harry. It's my turn, that's all."

"Are you sure?" My longing to stay, to hear her again, made me anxious. I had to ask it twice: "Are you sure?"

"Yes, of course. We still need you."

So I stayed on; and she kept playing.

She was cooking again now, so that each evening when

he came home Danny would fill his glass and then boom the house full of Wagnerian torment, letting the sound fill the thick walls of the living room and leak out into the dark night under the chestnut trees, and then, when Ebie called us to supper, he would shut it off.

Sometimes she would have a glass of red wine with the meal, but mostly she stuck with her coffee. Danny never drank after dinner.

We had our routine. Each evening I would come into the kitchen and offer to help. Then I would ask: "Don't you think it's time I went on? Left you two alone?" I would mention the new quarter, setting the date always just a week or so away. (I had no intention of getting back in school that spring, if ever, but I wanted to sound as if I had concrete options.)

"Wait, Harry," she would say. "Wait a little longer." And she would turn and look right at me, and I would nod.

Then Danny would come home, we would eat, have our sweet, hot tarts, and start up a fire in the grate.

On weekends, now that she was able, we would some-times take a drive to nearby Penyrile State Park to see the stand of pine trees and look at the lake where families came to swim in the summer. It was past hunting season, which was allowed on the grounds, but not yet warm enough for campers, so we had the woods all to ourselves. We sat in sweaters, our shoes in pine needles, our cheese and bread from home on the picnic table, and watched the red birds, and the steam rising from our hot thermos of coffee. We would stay until the moon rose in the early evening sky and then drive back. "Harry here likes the out-of-doors," he would tell her.

But either way, after supper or after our outing, she would give us time to get settled, and then she would play.

And that was the best part of all.

After a few weeks of this, she brought up the dog again. "Papa's got a dog in there which he never lets out. He's gone senile, Danny. It's stinking up the place."

"When wasn't he senile? You're having your dreams again—"

"Papa's nephew wrote me today. He said Papa had locked himself up in there with a dog and wouldn't come out. They want to declare him, to put him in the county home."

"You don't have to get permission to lock up Grade A lunatics." Danny had begun to boil.

"They bathe you there," she said. "They feed you."

"Well, let them, then. Take the mongrel, too. Dip them both. They've got my permission."

She looked across the room as if through the wall. "I have to go down to see about it."

Danny grabbed her chin and jerked her around facing him. We were still at the table, a dust of sugar on our plates. "No!" he bellowed. "No! You're not going back to that godforsaken swamp again."

"It isn't, you know."

I wasn't sure what she meant.

"You like to didn't get out the first time, and you lost Bea and almost got yourself killed to boot the second. I've got superstitions the same as anybody. Third time is hex. Your old man puts a curse on you as soon as you get in smelling distance of the Cotton Valley outskirts."

"His hexer's broken." She began to clear the dishes. "He

can't read. He doesn't send out the tax mailings to his membership anymore. He's locked in that house with a dog which messes on the floor and they have nothing to eat but what Papa's nephew sticks through the back screen."

"Had any sense, he'd stick roach powder."

"You carried *your* daddy," she reminded, ominously calm.

"It was due," he said flatly.

It was the old refrain again.

Angry, Danny stood up—which never got him far. "Let them find him and the dog, a couple of skeletons, and fifty years of tax dollars stuffed in the commode. Make all the papers: lunatic millionaire dies like a half-wit in the swamps of Louisiana."

"They aren't swamps." Ebie lost her temper. "It was all right for you to drive all day and all night across those winding roads, leaving me here, to set your old daddy in the backyard and then turn around and drive home. Year after year because he was too mule-stubborn to live with us, and too mean to be taken in by his own brothers. Leeching the blood out of you, that's what he did."

Getting to my feet, I murmured, "Might as well make myself useful around here." I started in to wash the dishes, which she let me do sometimes, and which Danny had let me do all the time.

"Wait, Harry." Ebie called me back. "Let's play. Together. You pick the music; I'll accompany."

My feet didn't want to move for a moment, but it seemed more an asking for help than a command, and, besides, piano teachers did accompany their pupils sometimes. So I nodded. At least it would ease things. I'd noticed that since she got home she'd lost her tolerance for Danny's outbursts.

We went through the music, and decided on the last of Beethoven's Seventh Sonata. We did a little shifting around, but it sounded good. Danny almost wept, his anger gone; so we played it again for him, better this time.

Then I excused myself and took a walk, which I did unless it was raining, which was most of the time. I had begun to do that since she got home; to warm up to becoming a naturalist, and to leave them alone.

An earlier thunderstorm had soaked the lawns and streets, mashing the violets which had pushed up through the mulching leaves and spring grass. Trees still dripped water, and the old streetlamps were repeated in a dozen pools.

What nagged at me that night, as I strolled under a sky fat with clouds blown apart by the wind, was what she had said about the letter from her father's nephew. I had brought the mail in, as I was expecting remuneration from my folks—who showed an almost minimal pleasure that I was on a semester's work-study program in the slums of Paducah, Kentucky—and there had been no letter from Louisiana. I'd checked every envelope.

Maybe he had called?

But I knew he hadn't. In fact, sometimes I got the idea that there was no cousin, that "Papa's nephew" was the name Ebie gave to her second sights, to what she saw when she looked down the road to what hadn't happened yet. Or that's how it seemed that spring, in the dark yard where impassioned music still clung to the dripping trees.

When I got back, they had gone to bed. I played the

Beethoven again, very softly, to make an echo of it, in case they could hear.

It had been a good night, one of the best we had together. And the last.

In the morning she was gone.

It was I who found the note she left for Danny on the kitchen table.

> *I have to go back.*
> E.

He went crazy. I had to wake him to tell him, it was that early. I don't know how she got up and out of there. I had an image of her in a nightgown getting soaked on the wet streets, bathrobe and coat on top, suitcase in hand.

Danny decided she must have taken the bus, as there wouldn't be anything else going into that godforsaken swamp. But when he called the bus station in Cotton Valley, he got a cretin with cobwebs for ears. His words.

"Don't no buses stop here, mister."

"Isn't this the goddamned bus station?"

"Don't no buses stop no more. We sells Hallmark Cards here now."

"What?" I thought they could hear him in the next county.

"Train stops at Minden, you wants the train."

He tried the train, but it was freight only.

We asked the Paducah Greyhound station for routes through Little Rock, Pine Bluff, Hope. We got the jumping-off places of planes. It seemed that you couldn't get there from here.

I don't know why I didn't think, since I'd heard the

story, that if Shreveport was where she left from, that's where she'd go back. And if she'd walked part of the way to run off from Cotton Valley, then she'd walk part of the way to go home. There was that kind of thinking in Ebie's mind.

She liked to tie up loose ends.

Which I guess is why she played Danny those final concerts.

Danny

————————◆————————

T H E first night Ebie went back into the hospital, sick, Danny got drunk out of his mind. He smashed a glass on the bathroom floor and threw another into the tub, and had to clean up the goddamned slivers without the kid downstairs hearing it. Which sobered him at least.

It drove him crazy at times like that to have a chaperon in the house. That had been Ebie's doing, because she knew what was good for him and what he needed to get along, and she was right—it would have been worse to be here by himself. And most of the time being sociable with Harry took the edge off her being gone, the way she had planned it to do, but some of the time it drove him stark crazy.

The only time he did fine was in the middle of the night, after he'd done with missing her and was on the verge of sleep: then he'd make that long drive back to West Virginia in his mind. For nearly a year now he'd done it every night. It might be he'd be making that drive the rest of his life. Some men counted sheep; he went back.

First he'd pass the grassy knolls and the big black silos rising up out of old hillocks, and the decrepit barns and granaries sagging halfway into the ground, abandoned and vine-covered, then creeks and wood fences, goldenrod and Queen Anne's lace, and fields of yellowing tobacco, and then as it got dark he would hit the limestone road-beds and begin to climb. He'd pass the little truck stops with Peterbilts parked for coffee, then the farms growing pigs and chickenhouses, making money off four-legged and two-legged things when they couldn't make money out of the dirt itself. Then, climbing into the black mountains where, when they couldn't grow it and they couldn't get feed off it, they had to dig down and sell the damn guts of the mountains themselves. He hated the fringes of the coal-mining area, although the highway bypassed anything to offend the eye; so that tourists seeing lush rolling land didn't have to notice that every few years it rolled a little bit lower. (When they got serious about strip mining and liquefying, all of eastern Kentucky and western West Virginia would be a grassy prairie—but that would be after his time.)

Then the fog would set in and he would grip the steering wheel—in his bed, on the brink of sleep—and jerk his nodding head, careful not to get drowsy or skid, nowhere to go with the dark valleys down below, Coopers Rock and East Coopers Rock, Fair Chance and South Fair Chance (towns segregating their blacks with an E. or a So. in front of the wrong side of town, taking their cues from the big cities, like No. Little Rock or W. Memphis). He would recall how it had felt to play football in high school while it was still dark as outside now, in the pea-soup-thick morning fog, him and Threkeld battering against each other till they warmed up and got awake.

And he'd be home. Cheat Lake: dingy little town nestled between Poorhouse Hill and Nigger Hill, lush with moss and vines and trees that you never got tired of looking at. And he'd remember everything: the Catholic church, where all the girls you wanted to go with went but you couldn't; the Baptist church, which had big revival signs reading SEVEN PRAYERLESS DAYS MAKES ONE WEAK; the Free Evangelist, which was the one his old daddy had elected never to darken the door of; and Angela Gloriaski, whose sweater he had got off a dozen times before Threkeld caught him at it.

He didn't forget any of it.

None of it. No one. He never let any of them go. He had pictures of his mother and daddy when they were young, as young as Harry, but married and with him on the way. Pictures of Threkeld and the rest of them at football practice in the spring; of Angela on the steps of St. Anne's.

He could remember it as if it was right that minute, the minute of getting home each time and the minute of gripping the steering wheel in the bed on the flat edge of sleep. He could hear again his daddy shouting after his first stroke: "I can't feel my hands with my face. I can feel my face with my hands, but I can't feel my hands with my face."

Danny had carried him to the doctor.

Later he'd carried him to the backyard.

And to the doctor's again, for almost a dozen years.

Then, last Easter Sunday, before Ebie had a baby coming, Danny had carried him to the undertaker.

He remembered his daddy standing outside looking at the sky, saying: "Gonna snow. We'll have to put on the chains." And the woman down the street, her, too, the one who cooked for his daddy after Danny's mother died, and after he couldn't do it for himself, the batches of Italian "gravy" as she called the tomato sauces that left a good smell in the house.

His daddy had lived his short life a good man. (Or, as he had joked at the last, when he knew he was going, "I lived my good life a short man, Dan.")

They'd be making a country club out of the area any year now. That was what happened when the land gave out: they turned it into a resort. Just when a town would begin to eat the dandelions out of its yards, and give up eating chickens to have the eggs, and those who could got out, then the next you knew it would be a boat harbor or a golf club. That was the way progress happened. Turn a profit out of hunger. When there aren't young people enough left to wrestle a football in the fog, it's time to build a country club.

His daddy kept up with progress; he would have been right there, promoting the idea.

The last time, he carried his old daddy to the cemetery on the hill. He didn't go back again, and never would.

Except at night, on the brink of sleep.

He couldn't stand it when Ebie wasn't there. Half awake as the first daylight came in, he'd reach for her. Then remember. While she'd been in the hospital was bad, but this time was worse. He didn't know where she'd gone.

The only way he could deal with what she'd done was to decide that it must not have been his. She would think that worse than giving a baby away, to bring up one that wasn't his under his nose. If it was somebody else's, then she'd done what she had to do. She'd told the hospital that it had no daddy; so that must have meant it wasn't his.

When he could convince himself of that, it enabled him to shut the subject tight away in his head.

While she was in the hospital having an infection, he'd go for visitors' hours, twice a day, on the way to work and on the way home. Then he'd fix a mess of something for himself and the boy to make a meal of, and then, when he'd settled himself with a little music and asked the boy if he'd like to play his fiddle, he'd excuse himself and come upstairs.

To break a glass or, if he couldn't hold out, to call Louise. "What made her do it?" he'd ask. Or, "You're a nurse, is she going to get well?"

"Listen, Dan, I'm not on her case. She's got a full shift around the clock."

"I should have got them to call you in."

"She'll be all right. Take it easy. She wouldn't like that."

He would agree. "I needed to ask is all, if you knew."

Other times he'd make Louise mad, which was not his intent, for they went a long way back.

"You going to stay with the baby-sitter until your wife comes home?" she would complain.

"It's right that I be here."

"I can't believe you're acting meek as a lamb with your baby taken off by strangers. Ebie's tamed you like a sheep, Dan."

"It can't be mine is what I decided."

"Whose, then? Not the boy's, not his, surely, right under your nose?"

Danny thought that was funny. Because Ebie knew she was already pregnant before they went out there. She had told him. No, she told him in Colorado, but before they met Harry. Besides, that was a crazy idea. "You're crazy," he said. He didn't know how to say it to Louise, but he knew that there were reasons that that couldn't be right. He knew that the boy, for one thing, hadn't grown up enough to notice girls. Some it took a while. It had taken Threkeld about five years after he married to get the idea—so he'd heard from Angela, who ought to know.

His problem was he couldn't let any of them go. He had to hang on to all of them. When he'd taken Ebie to live with him and married her because she was unstable and couldn't take care of herself, he'd tried to let Louise go. She had her work, worked time and a half most days. She didn't want kids, and was glad to see him take up with Ebie. Or so she said.

But he couldn't let go. When she showed up in Paducah he hadn't minded. She reminded him of his mother and Angela and a lot of the women in Cheat Lake: getting a little heavy, liking to work, liking to get with a man, being positive. That was the main thing, that when a bad day came along they had a way of taking it in stride. "God never promised not to rain on your picnic," his mother liked to say.

Louise, in reminding him of home, had a place in his life. Whenever Ebie went off too far, or when he got to missing those years of football practice and trying to get at Angela, he'd call Louise.

When he'd had the baby, Bea, he hadn't remembered Louise as much, and she'd tell him about other men, and he thought of her as more of a friend. In those days he was busy wondering if some of his mother's ways would seep into his little girl the way traits did, by osmosis, by the way you laughed or slapped your knee when they did something that reminded you of what you liked a lot. That's what heredity was, them reminding you and you letting on that you liked it.

And that was the way it had worked: something that was not Ebie had rubbed off on Bea. She was a flirt from the word go. Always taking her panties off when they had company; or eating with both hands and wiping the mess all over her face and giggling to get attention. She'd wake up in the morning raring to go, waking him, waking Ebie, waking the neighbors if she felt like it, running outside in those little pajamas with the feet in them.

When he had carried her sick to the hospital he'd laid his cheek against hers and it was hot as a furnace. Then it was he who couldn't feel his own face with his hands—for the tears.

Way down out of sight where he couldn't see it and dig it out to look at it was the suspicion that this last baby hadn't been someone else's at all, but that Ebie was running from having another. That she didn't want to get attached again in case something cruel should happen. She might have reasoned that she'd snap in two if she tried to raise another, coming as she did from Grade A lunatics.

But when he entertained that thought, or even the fringe of that thought, such a rage would fill him that another little Bea was going to bounce on the knee of some fool like Threkeld who never knew what he had his hands on, that he would smash his glass on the tile, finding it unbearable. Unbearable and stupid of her to take on herself to decide what he could have decided for himself. Sometimes he would content himself with throwing a pillow at the lamp or beating the bed with his fists, and would have done worse but for the presence of the boy downstairs below.

The same way he tried to let go thinking of the baby, taking Ebie's word for it that there was a reason, he now tried to quit thinking about tracking her down to Cotton Valley. Her note didn't say right out that's where she was, back at the lunatic's. It just said: *I have to go back.*

Maybe she'd gone off with the father. In which case it wouldn't be permanent. She might have found out about Louise and be getting even. That was fair, if she went off for a time to get back at him. But she wouldn't have needed to do more than that. She wouldn't have needed to give up the baby.

At the remembering he would fly into a rage.

Both at that and at the fact that she was gone. He didn't like her gone.

When the phone rang he was holding the pillow to his face, fighting an urge to bawl.

"Danny, is that you?"

"Jesus Christ. Ebie. I'm out of my mind. It's been four days. Didn't you realize—?"

"I shouldn't of come. I made a mistake."

"Where are you?"

"Papa's. They tore out the climbing glories. . . ."

"I'm coming down to get you."

"No. I'll come. I'll come the way I came."

She hung up.

Danny tried to get the operator to trace the call. But the operator was unable.

He rifled through his mind about how to call her daddy. There was a hitch to it, a roundabout way to get to the lunatic, who had an unlisted phone, but he was so riled up he couldn't call it to mind. It took a minute to calm down and remember. There was a phone in the house, he knew that, so Cothron could talk to his network of other loonys around the country. That crazy paranoid. How did he have it set up? It wasn't unlisted, that would be impossible in a little town anyway, but it was in some lunatic name. Was it Christian Tax Evaders? American Commies For Paying No Taxes? Jesus. He was too worked up to remember.

He looked in the dresser where he and Ebie kept their bills and the like. He found in Ebie's hand her Cotton Valley address. Like she might have forgotten the house she grew up in and almost didn't get out of. In a town that size. Like she might have forgot it was Elm and got mixed up and thought it was Maple. He couldn't figure her out. But no phone number. He tried to think of the nephew's name, but it was just nephew, that's all she ever said, Papa's nephew.

He was at his wits' end when he remembered the cretin at the bus station which now sold Hallmark Cards. In a town that size, everybody knew everything.

By this time Danny had come downstairs and got the boy at his elbow, to help him out.

"Is this the bus station?"

"Don't no buses run here, mister."

"Goddamn it, I know that. You told me. You sell cards now. Is this the place?"

"We sells gifts, too. For ever occasion."

"Good. You're the one. Tell me how do I call that lunatic who lives locked up like a hermit on Elm Street by himself and runs the mail-order operation? You know who I mean, Cothron Brewster. Old man Brewster." Not that Danny knew if Ebie's father was old, never having laid eyes on him, but anybody walled up that long sure wasn't young.

"You mean Mr. Brewster the one who never come out?"

"That one."

"I asks Mrs. Parker." She was gone from the phone the length of time it takes to sing the National Anthem three times. Danny could hear humming in the background and busying around. Finally she was back. "I told her you wants to get in touch with Mr. Brewster. She used to be Central here. She knows."

An old woman gave out the news that the hermit had gone from bad to worse and that rumor had it that he got a dog locked up in there with him stinking to high heaven and wasn't that the last of pea time for such a man as that?

Danny got himself under control. "Do you know how he lists his telephone, ma'am?" He could see he'd have to go through the pleasantries. "As I recall, it's out of the ordinary."

"If he still operates it the way he used to—I was the Central for forty years—"

"Yes?"

"It was cotton, that's what it was."

COTON. Of course. Danny had forgotten the secret code: Just call Coton in Cotton Valley. It said that on the letterhead. That was an acronym spelled backwards, to keep the feds at bay. NO TAXATION ON COMPENSATION. NOTOC. COTON. It took a Grade A lunatic to design something like that.

"Thank you, ma'am. You've been a big help. Jogging my memory."

"Your wife should of stayed run off, if you ask me."

"If you ask me, too." Danny should have known that she knew who he was. That was the essence of wide spots in the road. Omniscience. He hung up gently on the former Central, thanking her again, feeling he'd been civil past the point of endurance.

Well, he couldn't very well tell Operator to ring COTON for him. He felt like a fool. He might as well call and tell them to ring DADDY in Cheat Lake.

He wanted to say: "Dial lunatic for me, lady. That's L-U-N . . ."

Harry took over for him. He got the directory, called information for an exchange number, translated the code word into digits, and in a matter of seconds, had told some operator to place a call to TE 2-6866, Cotton Valley, Louisiana.

In his present state, he felt like the boy had worked a miracle. Gratefully, he took the receiver.

A voice in his ear said: "That line doesn't answer, sir. You may place your call again later."

"Is it ringing? What's happening?"

"That line doesn't answer at this time, sir. You may place your call later."

"What's going on?"

"That line seems to be out of order, sir. You may try again at a later time."

He hung up the phone in a fury of frustration. It was the last and final lunatic straw. Maybe the fool had sold COTON at the local exchange. Maybe he'd been dead for ten years and the drugstore now had that number. Maybe he'd been dead long before she buried her mama. How did Danny know? Maybe she never even came from Cotton Valley. What proof did he have? He took a deep breath and noticed that Harry was handing him a generous glass of whiskey.

He tried to calm down. The Central for forty years at the National Anthem-playing Hallmark Card bus station had definitely told him his wife shouldn't have come back, and that the old man was the last of pee time. Definite confirmation of true facts.

He had to sit down. He and Harry went into the living room. To calm down he played Wotan's Farewell. It sounded faint to his ears, having to get past the roar of his anger. He could hardly hear it and had to keep turning it up, but he could see the boy get that pained frown that came from its being too loud. "You'll give me deafness," Harry would say, and Danny would apologize.

You needed someone around for that. If he was by himself and couldn't hear it he'd think something was wrong with the machine. This way he knew something was wrong with his attention instead. It was; it was listening for the phone.

Finally it rang. Harry didn't hear it above the voices, but Danny was up in a flash, shouting: "Where are you?" before there was a sound at the other end.

Harry cut off the record player and stood at his side.

"What? Who is this?" Some man was talking and none of the words were getting through. Danny tried to get a hold on himself.

"Armistead. Honestly, I didn't know she was coming. You have to believe me. It wasn't my doing. If I figured it was my fault, I would . . . Honestly, you have to . . ."

"Who?"

"Armistead. You know, Ebie's cousin, Armistead Brewster. Her daddy was my uncle. I'm sure she's mentioned me—"

"What are you talking about?"

"I didn't know she was coming. I didn't send for her. I want you to know that, you have to believe me, sir, Mr. Wister, I guess I should say. I told her not to go in there with him, but she would. I told her. I'm a happily married man, for the second time, bless the Lord, as my first marriage was not a joyful one, but I try to do right. I wasn't one to complain, I try to take whatever the Lord sends me in the right spirit. I told her not to go in there with him. He had got demented. I figure that's a true description of the facts. He had a hound in there, I don't rightly know how long, or what exactly he fed it. I know that Red Circle Grocer, whose son is now running the place, and not as lenient about charging and delivering as his old man, not that I blame him, the town's growing, but he told me that there wasn't enough food going in there to feed one human, much less a dog, and no dog food, he told me that." The man took a couple of deep gulps while Danny tried not to holler out and get the connection cut off.

"I figured we'd get him to a home." The nephew, or cousin, continued in his mousy whine: "If she would sign the papers, I figured we could do that, and that would put an end to it. He's not been right in his head for twenty years, if you want my truthful opinion, although he's kin and I've no right to say it. But I never figured he was fully demented, not so as to do away with the both of them, the dog as well, not that that counts. I want you to know that I didn't know she was coming. I played no part. I told her not to go in . . ."

"What's happened to Ebie?" Danny could feel his head about to pound off his neck. He wanted to take this piss-ant and break his cousinly, nephewly neck into very small matchsticks and light them and shove them sequentially up his weasel ass. What was he saying? "What are you saying?" He turned to the boy and bellowed: "What is he saying?"

Somebody needed to interpret. The news was like the Wagner: he could barely hear it, his ears were full of roaring. It made no sense, he wanted to turn the volume up, the pipsqueak off.

"Must of locked it and set fire, that's all we can figure. Must of locked it tight, the firemen couldn't do nothing but stand back and watch it, the County Volunteer Fire. No sign of anybody trying to get out. Must of locked it tighter'n a drum. Him and her and that starving hound dog. I didn't figure he was in full possession of his faculties, but I wouldn't of said he was demented."

"Is she dead?"

"I called as soon as I saw that nobody come out. I don't rightly know, Mr. Wister. All I know is we had words, and then I saw her go in there."

"How long ago?"

"She was kindly upset, and said she'd just tell her papa goodbye and get herself back to Minden. Which was something I wouldn't of allowed. My intentions were to drive her to Shreveport to catch a Greyhound. My wife was understanding, it being kinfolk that had come down. I figured we could get my uncle in a home, the county home, if she'd sign, but I never meant—" His voice trailed off.

Danny let me take the phone and hang it up.

He told me to call the Hallmark bus station, that those ladies would have hotfooted it over to Elm and raked the ashes by now. If there was his wife in there, they'd know it beyond a doubt. Like Central said, she should have stayed run away. Danny tried to get it into his head. What was clear was that she had gone for good. She'd gone and given away her own goddamned self this time, without so much as letting him know.

Throwing back his head, he began to howl like a dog.

Harry on Harry

I loved him. You only do that once, let go and love with all the stuff you've been saving since childhood, never having had a place to put it. You carry it around with you until your shoulders bend with the weight of it, and then when you find someone who deserves it, down it comes, all of it.

Danny was father, son, and Yellow Dog to me, all rolled into one.

My first thought when we heard about Ebie's death was that it was my place to stay and take care of him. That we would remember always that year as the one where she had slipped farther and farther away from reality until she gave first her infant away, and then herself, a victim of her beginnings.

I envisioned that we would talk about it after a while, not bitterly, but sadly, that she had not been able to make a whole life away from her past, understanding that it must be too difficult to make a clean break when you have been so cloistered as a child.

I would stay and learn the names of the trees and rocks and animals, whatever would be required to become a naturalist. Danny would continue his physics. It made sense to me: *physics* must come from the same root as *physical*. I would bring to him the long walk, the observation of nature he had admired in his daddy, in whatever way would be a comfort to him. It was all somewhat vague in my mind, how that would be income-producing for me, but that was not something I was worrying about then. The need to stay, to be with Danny and look after him, was the point.

He'd gone upstairs in a state of shock. "I need to get some sleep," he said. "You get some sleep, too." He had a fresh glass of whiskey in his hand.

He had let me call the Hallmark ladies, but by that time there was no answer. I called the police station then, which shows that I don't know anything about country towns. "You may replace your call tomorrow," the Bell voice repeated. It seems police stations shut down like barber shops at six.

I waited. I would go up to him and help him get through the night.

First I played the Beethoven that Ebie and I had played together that last time. A sort of requiem. Very softly. So that he could hear it or not, depending on the state of mind he was in.

I had no idea what you did when you were grieving. In our culture there is the image of a lot of people hanging around cutting pies and telling old anecdotes. It came to me that Danny had had the same thing happen not long ago, "carrying" his old daddy to the undertaker. Maybe no one else was there with him then, not even the woman down the street who cooked. Maybe he had stood there and said, "Goodbye, Daddy," and turned around and made the drive back over the mountains alone.

He didn't have to do that this time. If he wanted to go down to Louisiana to stand over the remains of a crackpot old man he'd never met and a mummified dog and some ashes he believed to be Ebie's, I would go along. I would go with him tomorrow, drive all day, however long it took. I had no idea how far it was from Paducah, Kentucky, to Cotton Valley, Louisiana, not too far it seemed like.

(It made me really sick to my stomach to imagine being locked up in a house that was on fire and not able to get out. I had frantic images of throwing an iron through the window to get help, and nobody seeing. The panic when you saw what was coming would be almost worse than dying. Or so it seemed; it may be because I had just turned twenty and didn't know.)

We would go around and get the facts of the ordeal, what had really happened. I would talk to the cousin so that Danny wouldn't smash him in the nose. (I didn't know what he thought exactly, but he was definitely ready to kill the fellow.) I would interview the neighbors. We would make arrangements for a memorial service. Something perhaps where Ebie was buried beside her mother, with the Righteous grandfather, if he was there. The lot that the ashes and rubble were on could be sold. Anyway, it would all be swallowed up in vines, like you read about happening to whole hillsides in that part of the country, until the bad legend is covered over and quiet is all that's left.

Then we would come back here. I would see what I could do about college here, or close by. And gradually Danny would come out of it, heal over how it had been.

I'll admit it did cross my mind to wonder what he was going to do with himself without Ebie, when he'd kept his hands twisted around in her hair or fingering her sleeve all the time. But I remember that I told myself that his solicitude had been a response to her fragility and needy ways, and didn't come from his own insecurities or wants. Hadn't even I taken to looking after her at the end?

When the last notes had died down, I put the violin in its case, the bow beside it, and climbed the stairs.

I would not hesitate. I would hold him and comfort him the same way he had done his daddy. Metaphorically, I would carry him out into the yard in the sun. He had done that; now it was my turn.

As I approached the bedroom, I heard what sounded like something being thrown across the room, and then his voice, yelling and sobbing: "Goddamn it, Louise, you've got to come. I don't care, I can't stand it being here alone by myself tonight."

The next day I left.
Taking the marble bag with me.

3

Harry

———————◆———————

FIFTEEN years after the winter in Paducah, I had forgotten them all, or tried to. When Danny promptly married
the nurse, Louise, I didn't stick around to catch any further
developments. From time to time I kept in touch, but that
was all. I'd had enough of doing all the grieving single-
handed to last a lifetime.

I became a naturalist after all. Neither because of Danny
nor to spite the Roses K., but because of a chance copy of
Fabre's Book of Insects and its loving glimpse into nature's
workshop:

> For forty years it was my dream to own a little bit of
> land, fenced in for the sake of privacy: a desolate, bar-
> ren, sun-scorched bit of land, overgrown with thistles
> and much beloved by Wasps and Bees. . . . And that is
> why I deserted the town for the village, and came to
> Sérignan to weed my turnips and water my lettuces.

Which is what I longed for most: a remote terrain whereon
my only cares were noting, weeding, and watering.

Which isn't how it was, naturally. At that time my goal
was to become a museum curator in some first-class natural-

history museum. Out of college, I'd worked a while in Aspen, familiar turf, taking hikes and tours around Pitkin County and environs in the Rockies; then I'd done the Big Bend National Park in Texas. By the summer of 1981 I was working my way up the Taconic State Park Commission hierarchy in a good job that combined public-relations sessions trying to persuade the Rockefellers to donate twenty-five hundred acres of Hudson River Valley to the park system, and taking Westchester residents on nighttime animal-tracking treks around nature preserves, and daytime geological walks on nearby glacial moraines. I enjoyed both parts of my job, and meant to stay put a spell.

(The only echo from the past was my golden Labrador retriever, who spent most of her time burying tunafish cans in the backyard.)

But even if I had not, as Fabre did, repaired to an un-tilled, pebbly expanse of ground to grow thyme, tend grapes, and prune my tangle of arbutus, it was still a simple, retrogressive world that I inhabited. I might even have finally taken up the study of physics, had I been able to contemplate the Pulley and Lever as Fabre did his Wasp and Bee.

The summer I met Jeanetta Mayfield I was employed at Bennington College as assistant recreation leader in charge of nature for their Summer Arts Program. My job entailed taking teenagers on bird sightings and tree-identification strolls and owl hoots, the sum a thinly disguised way of providing minimal chaperonage for those who wanted to stumble off into the bushes together. The summer brochure invited students to bring binoculars, nets, and hiking shoes. Only the slow at heart could fail to read that message.

The reason for the low-pay, low-status summer diversion

was my infatuation with a nineteen-year-old called Jakob who reminded me of my past self to an amazing degree.

We met in Manhattan at friends' of friends'. He moved around totally at home, introducing people to each other, not getting stuck with anyone, making small talk with Aubusson-rug types and political anarchists alike. I was charmed, as at that age the only time I had relaxed was with persons with four legs.

"I'm Jakob Plover," he told me, "with a *k*."

I stared at him, taking in the trim smudge of beard, the clean fingernails and topsider shoes. "Bullshit." That was the only conclusion. "You're Cabot Lodge the Fourth. From Grosse Point."

He grew sullen. "Mark Kenelm Hopkins Williams II. Long Island. How could you tell?"

"Easy."

We sat in a corner by a stand of house plants, looking out at the Hudson River, watching it shimmer, drinking Amaretto and hearing each other against a loud backdrop of party mania. I told him I had once been Harrod Roncevaux, an alias now ten years deceased. He flushed, but he liked it. He admitted he thought he was the only nut in the world. Nineteen is like that.

"I used to tell people I lost my father in the bombing of Guernica."

"I lost mine to Bracket Creep."

We each waited for our joke to click, and then he asked was Guernica like Iwo Jima or something, and I had to inquire if bracket creep was kin to jock itch.

We came from different worlds. But he was spending time in a place I'd been, so that made up for it.

"How about your mother?" Rose K. mater didn't seem the type to fit with bracket creep.

"Her idea of cooking is to heat Grapenuts in the microwave."

"Some years I'd have settled for that."

"Now you're being condescending."

I didn't take offense; I was. "So where is Jakob from?"

"Plover is East European. Immigrant."

"I see."

"They always talk about rude day laborers, and my old man is rude, so I thought, why not?"

"Jewish?"

"Not exactly, because, you know, I don't know the holidays or all that food business."

"East European holidays you know?"

"You're putting me down again."

"I'm wondering if I was that obvious."

"You're pretty obvious now." His back was up.

"How so?"

"I mean, how many people walk through the door of apartments on the upper West Side in backpacks and hiking boots in the spring? You look like you might start yodeling any minute."

"It was worse in the days when it was a violin case."

"Music cases are heavy."

"That was the reason I switched."

"I'm a writer."

"You or Jakob?"

"I *am* Jakob."

"Sorry."

"I'm working on a novel these days, but I don't like to talk about my work."

156

Gently I bypassed that obvious lie. "How can Jakob's mom afford a microwave?"

"That's *mine*. His is tubercular."

"Nice. Goes good with immigrant."

"I don't see why you have to keep on being that way. I mean, what am I supposed to do? Nobody who actually went to Choate and is enrolled at U. VA. for God's sake, is going to get anywhere as a writer. I had to have another *persona* is all."

For some reason it all made me very happy.

By summer I had agreed to go to Bennington as a lover of bullfrogs and sugar maples so that I could watch M.K.H. Williams II, a.k.a. Jakob Plover, be the writing assistant to a woman poet who smoked cigars and wore floor-length caftans and presided, like a Valkyrie, at all readings and lectures. He went about in tattered pants and workshirts, his beard a deepening smudge and the bags under his eyes darkening in the summer sun. He had the afternoon class of kids who had taken poetry in the morning from the Valkyrie and didn't want flute or ballet or theatre in the afternoon, the real hard core who couldn't play anything but a pencil. Naturally, despite his efforts to be remote and discouraging, Jakob, who secretly thought every kid had a better talent than he did, soon had a feverish cult of groupies. As it humiliated him to be instantly popular, he chopped his hair off in 1940s prison-camp style.

I liked it that he thought he could carry all that off with such an obvious preppie accent—the Long Island way of being *modified* (mortified) at having to discuss *mocks* (marks) with his kids.

But the best times were when he gave me the daily installment of his Great Novel, which, to my surprise, did not turn out to be a saga of plague and inequality in East Europe, but simply a big *lock* (lark). "See," he would begin, "there are these two guys who drive a stolen load of frozen chickens . . ."

"The load is stolen, not the truck, right?"

"Right. It's a U-Haul and they begin to thaw going over the mountains of West Virginia . . ."

"The two guys, right?"

"Right. But there is worse to happen, one of them has shot his invalid mother with gold bullets and stabbed her to death and drunk her blood, so that's why they're on the lam, forming part of this one monotonous line of trucks in West Virginia. But he, the guy from Bois d'Arc, Arkansas, has a cast-iron alibi with Call Forwarding."

"Come again?"

"This business the phone company has, you know, where somebody can ring you up only they've been automatically switched to another number where you actually are. It's for businessmen who're screwing around, or real-estate ladies who don't want to miss a sale. Well, see, they call this person and have him call back, they say they're at home and he calls and gets them, so he thinks they're there, but they've switched the number and are talking from somewhere else while they search for golden bullets in the mother's wallpaper. See?"

"Meanwhile the chickens are thawing in the mountains?"

"That's the one guy's alibi, the one from Bois d'Arc, but the other, who's an accomplice, slips out and uses the Wall."

"I give up."

"You know, the Wall. The thing you stick your plastic card into and get money out. It tells you good day and your account balance. The way it works is only you know your secret banking code, you and the Wall. So nobody else but you could have been there; so the Wall gives you an alibi. You say, 'But look, officers, I was there at two fifteen p.m., pushing in my plastic card and pecking out my code word, HENS, which I wouldn't confide to you but I'm under oath, and I got a hundred, four twenties and two tens, for the weekend. My mother lives in the Hamptons.' So the police check, and, sure enough, you got your alibi."

I never tired of the plot. I was content. Nineteen revisited was grand, as uplifting as the Vermont air.

When we weren't at our respective classes, we pursued his novel, or talked about revenges against parents, and how to achieve same, with style.

I told him about the twenty-four-year-old who filed a suit asking $350,000 in damages against his mother and father because they had inflicted emotional distress on him by willfully neglecting psychological support at crucial times in his life. That story was at the top of the class in my fantasies of attention-getting.

"That's crass—" Jakob was revolted—"suing for money." His favorite was the story of professional atheist Madelyn Murray O'Hare's son, who found Jesus in his life on Mother's Day.

That did take the cake, and when there was a lull, I'd say: "Tell it to me again."

In the years when I was changing over from H. Roncevaux back to Harry James, I spent a good bit of time in the company of a fair-to-middling therapist who examined the evidence with me. The single line of his I remember was: we feel better with what is familiar.

The context of the remark escapes me, but its connection to this summer was clear: it was the damnable familiarity of Jakob's pose that I couldn't resist. I suspected but did not say aloud that if he ever became Mark Kenelm Hopkins Williams II full time again, and a graduate of U. VA. and a journalist, I wouldn't feel the same about him. It was in that connection, my own bout with the lingering virus of nineteen, that I told him about Danny.

Of whom he decided, quite needlessly, to be extremely jealous. For one thing, he decided that I was lying about what really happened in that winter in Paducah, which I wasn't; besides, it all seemed much ado about what was long ago. But that's the way I found the girl in the end; because Jakob knew the story.

As it turned out, she had been mentioned already in a couple of conversations, but we didn't make the connection then.

Once when we ate in the dining hall with the cigar-smoking poet in her lavender mumu, she told a story on herself:

"I was in a cab in the City when this cabbie asks me what do I do. 'I teach writing,' I say. Somewhat smugly, as we do. 'I always got A in penmanship myself,' he says, and proceeds to pass back a sample of his handwriting, very cursive and full of loops. 'I trace the letters in magazines,' he says, 'until I find a style I like.' " She stopped to let that sink in. "That put me in my place, all right."

A visiting writer picked up the theme, seeing a chance to name-drop. "I was with Styron," he said, "the day he told me he'd finished *Sophie's Choice*, we're at a party, a big bash, and this bimbo standing next to us, drink in her hand, smashed, says brightly: 'Oh, did you like it?' "

They laughed. Writers are like that, they love to tell anecdotes on themselves that remind them they lead coveted lives.

Jakob tried to continue in a vaguely similar vein, about his writing class. "I gave them this assignment, name the ten things you would most like to be called. I'm attempting to get them to act out of their feelings. So this one girl writes *limber*, and that's all she can think of. You know the rest of them, putting down things like *intransigent, exceptional, inscrutable . . .*"

"Don't tell me," the Valkyrie cried, "I know which one she is. The only one whose parents actually brought her to Bennington. I mean, half the kids here haven't seen either of theirs in five years or more. So we were talking with the parents, amazed they were here, and then we got off on Borges, a few of us, I can't remember the context, his blindness, the way he translates his own . . . Talking to pass the time. And this mother, this woman, who drives her dumpy blonde daughter all the way up here, pipes up with: 'I use Borghese cosmetics myself. . . .'"

"That's her!" Jakob bubbled at his success.

"Remember," the poet told him grandly, welcoming him into the inner circle, "this is a cultural experience for us, too."

"Your old lover's kid is here," Jakob announced two nights later. This was after my evening nature walk: past the bullfrogs, around the Music Building, along the dark, tree-lined road back to the Visual and Performing Arts Building, the while ostensibly noting stars. We were having a bedtime cup of coffee and sharing a blueberry muffin I'd saved from breakfast.

"My old lovers don't make kids," I answered, half listening. I was tired, and wanted, much as one does a late-night TV show, for him to bring us the day's installment of frozen chickens, thawing thieves, the monied Wall, the Call Forwarding alibi, the nimble drivers from Bois d'Arc, Ark. That, our end-of-the-day ceremony, constituted the bulk of the excitement of our summer at Bennington.

"One did. It must be his. I mean, how many adopted girls born fifteen years ago on Valentine's are there in Paducah, Kentucky?"

"About three hundred and fifty?" I conveyed disinterest as his words caught a hold of my midsection and held tight.

"Want to bet it's not?"

"How do you know her birthday?"

"I had them do bios for me, get them in touch with the material they already know; if they know their own backgrounds and the ten things they'd most like to be, they're half a writer right there. They did place in the family, class cues, all that. So that's how."

"Who is it?"

"I could have not told you." He wanted recognition for disclosure. Letting me know it was a painful subject.

"I doubt that. M.K.H. Williams II is at heart a Boy Scout."

He looked like he was going to go have a sulk in the shower, but he lay back and said, "The dumpy blonde: 'I want to be limber,' by Miss Stiff. The Borghese-mama kid. The worst writer in the class, if you want to know."

Which may have been why he told me, to show me I had bad taste in old friends.

"What's her name?" She must have been hiking around listening for owl hoots with me for half a month. Wouldn't I have known? Somehow?

"Jeanetta Edna Mayfield." He played the name like a trump card.

"That couldn't be her."

He let himself make a big Long Island smile. "Sure it is. The new parents do the naming."

Jeanetta? Had Ebie left her with a name? B. Righteous Wister? I didn't want to think of Ebie standing in her robe in the drafty living room of that house in Paducah, bleeding the residue on the rug, saying: "I gave her away."

"Come to my class and see."

"If it is her, she's been here all the time, holding hands with some big-bottomed gropie musician-type, hasn't she? Anyway, how can you tell something like that? I never know what people mean when they say, 'he looks like Uncle Ned.' What it is they see. No baby looks like Uncle Ned, or every baby does. For that matter, I'm not sure I could spot the child of my own parents walking down the street. Could you?"

"You can see for yourself." He pushed Waspishly at his clean, chopped-off East Europe hair. He needed to get full credit and he wasn't sure he was getting it. "I could have not told you."

"No, you couldn't; the suspense would have killed you."

So I did, I stopped by. Jakob finished the class each day with a page or two from the novel, to show them how work-in-progress progressed. How he used, I suppose, his ten-best list and his own (manufactured) class cues to weave a thick plot. The faces, twelve girls, two boys, were turned toward him, lasering worship. I'm not sure they heard him, but they saw the awe with which he read his own words aloud.

Reluctantly, I looked at each of them, expecting, halfway, to see Ebie look out from under a frame of black hair with eyes that grazed me with her glance as she searched our futures for what was there. Naturally, I didn't.

Most of them looked familiar, from two weeks of proximity, but none of them looked remarkable.

I shook my head slightly, then lounged against the doorway. I liked seeing Jakob do his show.

They clapped wildly when he finished and then bolted past me, dragging with them packs, hats, shawls, poems, pallor (the whole world of disguise). Except this one girl: when she rose, the last to leave, she appeared still to be sitting down.

When I saw the pink shorts riding full of hope on Danny's stubby legs, my heart broke in recognition.

"That's her?" I asked Jakob, when she'd gone.

"I told you."

Jeanetta. What a name. Surely she'd make up a better one.

Harry and Jeanetta

"I used to live in Paducah myself."

"That's what Jakob told me, he says to call him that. When I had my conference with him, he said he had a *friend* who lived down there once. I knew he meant you."

"How did you know that?"

"I have a lesbian acquaintance, Miss Beasley. It was her idea for me to come here."

"I see." I took a deep breath. "Are you one?" Harry James was careful not to smile as he strolled along under the giant fir trees, on the path past the slumbering bullfrogs, as beside him moved a girl whose walk he knew from a former life.

"Not unless it's hereditary. I don't know much about my heredity. I'm adopted. My real father was a doctor."

Jakob had related that already, that she'd put down that as well as what her present daddy did. I said that's not Danny, assuming they wouldn't mean a Ph.D. doctor, but Jakob said, "Come on, every adopted kid's father is a doctor. Didn't you know that? That's part of what you get when you adopt. What do you want them to tell the prospectives? That this grease monkey knocked up a car hop and they had to get rid of the kid? Every couple who places a child were both of them Phi Beta Kappas with good mental health and beautiful eyes, who simply had to leave the child in good hands because of religious differences, or the work of both becoming doctors—"

"I think I knew him," I told Jeanetta Mayfield.

"Really?"

I let that soak in.

"Could he curl his tongue?"

"What?" I was dumbfounded.

"It doesn't matter." She walked along, two steps for my one. "Did you know the girl he was in love with?"

"Uhh—?"

"My mother. That he couldn't marry."

"Ummm. No."

"That's all right."

Harry walked along in silence. We were climbing the old road that winds to the ridge where I often walked to hear the sound of practice pianos coming out of upstairs windows and get a breathing spell. It reminded me of the first blush of early Aspen, with music floating out second-story windows, the sound of summer practice drifting out over the meadow below.

I got overcome with a need to tell her everything I knew, how the grapefruit set in the west, about the printed cotton marble bag which I still had with its sixty cents. All of it, starting with the first hotplate supper, or, earlier, with the cream pitcher in my windbreaker pocket, which I could feel again at that moment. (Jakob was sick of it all. "You've told me a thousand times this week how she burned up. Maybe she lit the match because you were doing it with Danny.")

I crammed my hands into my pockets. Did you know my mother, the girl he couldn't marry? How we do make up our pasts. My old man bombed at Guernica; Jakob's mother a frail tubercular. It must be that it's too unbearable to know that there is no competition and you've lost anyway.

I, Harry, bit my tongue.

"That's all right," she said again when I didn't answer. "I mean, I only just found out, so that's been a long time. I expect they went back to leading their former lives and all, or maybe they moved away and put it all behind them."

"We do that," I said. Jeanetta's words had unleashed all my old memories. "Who told you?"

"Daddy and my mom," she said. "I mean, that's what they are. I guess I should say the Mayfields to you."

"How come they waited so long?"

She looked down as we reached the level road which starts to curve toward the trees at the Music Building. "I don't—" she concentrated but came up with nothing— "know." She looked at her shoes. "I guess they thought it was time because I was becoming grown."

"Are you their only child?"

"Yes. I guess they just wanted one."

"I'm an only child, too." I weighed that. "A lot of people pretend they're adopted. Did you ever do that?"

"No, but Leslie, she's my best friend, says that all the time—that she wishes she was. But she doesn't mean it. She means that her mom gets on her nerves. Her mom has a plant show on the radio and that embarrasses her because the kids at school hear it or pretend to."

"Does your mother get on your nerves?" I let my mind drift to mine, who did.

"We're really close, my mom and I. I tell her almost everything."

"I guess it's a good thing it was you and not Leslie who found out."

"She says she'd be glad, that I'm lucky." Jeanetta then decided that I was making a joke, and laughed. "You're the one who has the nature walks, aren't you?"

"Yeah. How come you don't join us?"

"Because that's not why the kids go on them."

"So?"

"You don't mind?"

"That's why I'm here: what they required was someone who would lead walks in the dark and look the other way."

"They didn't." She thought that was funny.

"So why don't you come? We take this very walk some nights." I stopped her so we could listen to the sound of a piano coming from the upstairs room, and, downstairs, the sound of a solitary flute.

"I practice in there," she said, pointing.

"That's not you playing now."

"No. You'd know if it was me; I play really loud."

"And you're in Jakob's prose class. Do you write loud?"

She laughed. "I'm the worst one in there, he says so. I don't know at all what I'm supposed to do, the way the other kids do. I can't explain it because you don't know me or anything, but you would think it would bother me, not to be good, but it doesn't because I know why, I'm not limber enough. When I told Jakob that, he laughed, but he didn't see that it was true. I used not to be able to see that for myself, but now I can, so the Summer Program has helped me a lot."

I had this vaguely sick feeling, imagining how Jakob would ridicule such a testimonial. She was literal, and if there's anything Long Island types and their cohorts in mumus can't handle, it's literal. I was reminded of the cab driver who was a beautiful *writer*. It made me mad, their attitude, for her.

"How do you like it up here in the north woods?"

"Everybody's friendly," she assured me.

"Even in Jakob's class?"

"He reads us from his book at the end of the period, and that's the best part."

It was a pattern: she simply turned away from the painful question, moved ever so firmly a few inches to the side so its point didn't pierce.

"How do you like *You Haul?*"

The novel now had a definite title, a definitive title. "Because of the U-Haul truck and then how you have to carry your own weight. Get it?" Jakob had sat up half the night settling on the title; he'd got to the point where he couldn't write another line without it decided upon. "You have to know where you're going; at some point the form requires a name." He had got to that point. I made my own suggestions: *Micro Wave*, for a small farewell, and *What Do You Want, Wall?* for the credit-card caper, and life. He had got angry and accused me of being intentionally shallow, the worst possible offense. "You always get shallow on purpose when we talk about my novel, it's your way of putting me down." He had wanted to name it *Call Forwarding* for the way we put off decisions down the road into the future, but that happened to be the name of the Bell Telephone pamphlet and he thought they might sue, or at least he'd have to worry about if it was a trademarked name. So *You Haul* it was, and we did, to sleep.

"He said his *friend* helped select the name."

"I asked you if you liked it."

"I don't—" She looked cornered. "I mean, it isn't finished."

I bit my tongue. The need to take over her education was getting the upper hand.

"Do you like it?" she asked (maybe to get a clue as to how to answer a question like that).

"I love it. I think all future literary criticism will date the novel from the year of the stolen load of frozen chickens."

"It sounds like you're making fun of him—"

"That's the very thing he says."

"But that's not nice."

"Then I must not be doing it, right?"

She was silent, rebuked. "Do you make fun of everyone?"

"Jakob says you're working with deaf folks." I imitated her dodge.

"I'm not going to tell you about it because you're not really asking, you're pretending to ask, and then you'll say something that will make me sorry I told you. A person can't be serious when they'll get laughed at."

"Do you think I'm that mean?"

"I think you're mad at somebody."

I took her pink oxford-cloth sleeve in my fingers and pulled her toward a stone wall beside the road. From there we could look out across a wide green field, back toward the campus proper and a forgotten collection of welded student artwork rusting in the sun. "I am," I admitted.

"At me?" She faced the open acres, her shoulder turned away from me.

"Not exactly."

"That's not fair. Whatever's the matter's not my fault. Did you have a fight with Jakob? Did he hurt your feelings?"

"The only way he could make me mad would be not to be nineteen anymore. I intend him to hang there on the cusp indefinitely, brooding in his East European way."

"Do you go around getting mad at your students? That's not very grown-up. Mr. Jenkins, my biology teacher, wouldn't do that."

"What would he do?"

"He would—" She smoothed her pink shorts and adjusted her barrettes. Defensive gestures. "He would—" She turned and looked at me, lost. "I don't know, if he was mad. We're not that close."

"Which means he's grown-up." I gathered that their not being close was not Jeanetta's idea.

"Why are you mad, then?" she asked me.

"It's not you." And what good did it do to be mad at them, those muddled people with their dead long put out of their minds? What good, from this point in time, here in beautiful, dull, rural Vermont?

She made a gesture of comfort. "I'm working with Deafs because they can hear a lot you wouldn't think they could, and even when they can't they get the idea. I may do it all the time when I grow up, like Miss Beasley, only I would do it with rhythm all the time."

I tugged her sleeve that it was time to get back. When we stood she said: "You're like the Deafs, doing that."

"It's hereditary," I said, choking up, finding it necessary to look away.

She became Yellow Dog all over again. (Which Jakob couldn't stand.)

As if by prearrangement, she would be waiting for me after lunch to take our frog-pond, high-ridge hike. Whereas at mealtimes in the cafeteria she would give us a quick smile over our muffins or stew, and that would be that. She had this sense of protocol.

"Miss Cake Mix, from Jelloville. I can't believe it." Jakob

fretted. "No wonder her old man sells Chevrolets. It fits."

"Life insurance."

"You think you'll get your lover back, that's what you think."

"He wasn't, and I don't. Besides, he has no idea where she is, and doesn't care." But I cared, and, naturally, Jakob sensed it. He was right: I wanted Danny to see her. Damn it, Danny, your own flesh and blood. You carried your old man around when his legs had withered, hung him outside to sun and air, folded him and put him back inside, weightless as a bedsheet. This is the same: kin. You blubbered like a baby over a kid dead a dozen years. You wouldn't let me get this one when we could still have had her. Damn it, Danny, I've found her for you; she's yours.

"That's all you've thought about since I said it was her. I wish I'd kept it to myself. I could have not told you, you know. You'd never have guessed. I practically had to put a name tag on her as it was."

"Deep in your heart, Mark from Bois d'Arc, you can't help it. You're fair-minded. It's the preppie trademark."

"I'm not having her hang around all the time. She doesn't even write about the deaf mutes, which is all she knows. 'How I Redecorated My Room for My Birthday.' The rest of them look out the window and snicker when she reads her stuff. She stands out like a freak. She absolutely doesn't have an original thought in her head. I don't see how you stand it. Next she'll be moving in with us. Well, that's when I'm moving out."

"The session will be over in a week. I'll take you to the Catskills and you can figure out what your heroes do to hide a stolen U-Haul van."

"Don't be snotty. Do not take my material and poke fun at it." He retired to the shower for an hour.

The bright spot for Jakob, and a peacemaker between us, was the Summer Program's star, the diamond in the necklace, the almond in the cluster of featured programs: Iris Murdoch.

Every weekend brought New Yorkers—primarily agents, editors, teachers, colleagues in the arts—come to beef up the program with readings, concerts, criticism, or perform-ance. No discipline wanted her/his art to go unheralded, or to appear lacking in luminaries. Sometimes these were closed sessions, available only to a particular class, in order to point out the teacher's intimacy with the artist and to enhance enrollment. Other times, expediency dictated that a particular flutist or novelist should have a large, respon-sive crowd, with all available students hanging on to the railings, sitting on the floor in the aisles, stomping and clap-ping and asking a lot of questions.

Such was Murdoch. She was the headliner; her name had been on all advance summer mailouts.

Jakob had mixed feelings about her appearance, as she was with her husband, critic John Bayley, and the format of their presentation wasn't clear. Jakob, fearful for his treasure, hated critics in advance of the fact, sure that they lay in wait to eviscerate the entire schema of frozen load and card-carrying alibi. (In my heart I knew he was wrong: his critics, inevitably from the same background of bracket-creep fathers and microwave mothers, would warm at once to the subliminal message of his light-hearted trek.)

Jeanetta was waiting for us, outside our apartment, at seven forty-five. It was, naturally, my idea that she accompany us. Nighttime shows, I assured her, were proper occasions to attend with teachers. It was hers that she wait outside and not intrude into my privacy with my *friend*. (Miss Beasley, wherever you are, let's someday have a long talk.)

As we trudged single-file, Jakob looked as if he could stomp a cake mix; he clutched in the direction of his windpipe every time she said anything. His modification (mortification) at being seen in public with her was evident to all.

(It had to do with class. You might want to change your name, shed every vestige of your parents' position, adopt a wild new identification, yet you could not, under duress, give up one single class signal that you had spent your life accruing. Could Jakob Plover have method-acted his part to the extent of going about in greasy hair and dirty underwear? Light-years before he could have donned maroon polyester pants and a white patent belt.)

It was that Jeanetta was dumpy and without pretensions.

But so, it turned out, was Murdoch.

I, expecting British, had assumed austere and brisk and wordy. Anyone who decides to be both novelist and philosopher and to marry a critic could be expected to appear in a coat of mail.

But down on the boards below us, gussying up to get ready to wander up to the podium, was this charmer in a baggy sweater and schoolgirl bobbed hair and round cheeks and big, flat washerwoman feet in what looked like bedroom slippers.

A beanpole man in a similar sweater, with sprigs of hair that stuck straight up, and a clear crush on her, propelled her to the speaker's stand. He put a glass of water in her hand, they bent their heads to say a few things, then she shook her head, he wagged his finger, and she was on.

The very sight made me pluck at Jeanetta's sleeve, in reflex.

"There you go," she whispered.

Iris had a large and captive audience and she played them off-handedly, making light of what was in fact a wry indictment against the self-indulgence of writers.

"When we return home from work, and relate our day, we shape rubble into story form," she said, peering up from under the lights at our dark forms crowding the bleachers. "One cheers oneself up, you see, by erecting form out of what would seem otherwise a senseless muddle. But when we write, we are too serious. Which dooms us never to be serious enough."

It's hard to say how much sank in. No group of artists likes to hear that it is playing when it thinks itself slaving, or working only when it feels itself off guard. Or that it can never get there, for the blockade, the mirror, which it puts to its face.

"Although it is true that the writer must be more than half in love with his unconscious, which does his work for him, at the same time he must not burden us with too much author. He must not be too bossy a presence." She looked up, a mole in a car's headlights, to be sure we were attentive to her point. "The great writer perceives the vastness of what is other than himself; he does not create the world in his own image. He describes an opening into the real world, a space we can explore. Most of us are fearful, obsessed, anxious, enclosed in our small personal worlds. The good writer shows us spaces, centers of reality which we cannot imagine for ourselves but perceive are true when we encounter them. His work gives us the memory of what we did not know we had. That is why we do not tire of great writing."

She talked for half an hour only, turning after every few sentences to look at the beanpole with the sprigs of hair, who would nod her on. When she finished, she picked up her notes and stuck them, and her hands, deep into the pockets of the baggy sweater, which came down almost to her knees.

"Thank you," she said when applause broke out, squinting up at us. She turned her back, looking for a way to leave.

Bayley came and tugged at the back of her sweater, to turn her around to us again.

Jeanetta whispered, "Look at that."

Murdoch nodded. Oh, yes, questions. She stared into the glare. Forty hands were up.

"Yes?" She leaned on the wood stand, interested that we still had something on our minds to say.

Which we did. Torrents of objections and accusations, couched, but not too artfully, as questions, poured forth.

"It is clear you are a victim of the 'realistic fallacy,'" someone accused. "We are sign-using animals who constitute ourselves and the world by our significance-bestowing activity. There is no world as you describe it which the artist opens to us. We live in a significance-world. If language makes the world, it cannot refer to the world." His voice rose in vexation at the end, to signify a question.

Murdoch replied: "Interesting. But the writer must not allow himself to be bullied by theories." She squinted at the top row. "Yes?"

"What do you think of structuralism, then? Could you please elaborate?"

Iris sighed and turned for help to Bayley, who nodded. "The structure of great literature," she said firmly, "has to do with erotic mysteries and the struggle between good and evil. . . . Next?"

It was Jakob, on his feet. "Are you saying, I hear you say, that literature written under the influence of a claque of formalist theories is writing for a select circle of cognoscenti?"

I hadn't heard her say that myself.

She blinked and nodded that she had heard. "The critical vocabulary I would direct against literature would be: is it untruthful? That's why we enjoy great literature: truth is always interesting."

Jakob looked defended, and Jeanetta and I were greatly relieved.

Murdoch threw up her hands and went to Bayley: this was not her field. He hadn't come along to speak, but she pulled him up there anyway. And he obliged. He stuttered, and at first, as he labored to get the syllables out, I thought it was going to be an awful mess. That's because I was the uninformed. Jakob related later that it was like watching a tennis match when you couldn't see the ball; John took every school of criticism and allowed it to self-immolate.

Pandemonium broke loose in little knotted areas, like hives. The rest of the audience—dancers, actors, musicians—yawned and considered that it might be all right to leave at that point. Someone took a hand-show on the number of vegetarian dinners for Tanglewood next week. One little girl, about four, brought along obviously in the absence of a sitter, tired of those old people being the center of attention, took her pants off and did a somersault in the aisle.

*   *   *

Jeanetta talked a blue streak. "Those people asking questions were talking so nobody could understand. The Deafs do that, make up a language that the staff doesn't know. Jokes they do with their hands." She waved her hand around and tapped on her head. "Bird-brains." She turned to Jakob. "Did you like Miss Murdoch?"

"It was highly satisfying. Her credentials are such that there could be no question of dismissing her views."

I translated: "He means yes."

Jeanetta looked at me with annoyance. "You don't have to tell me what Jakob says. He's my teacher, and I'm used to him. That was a sarcastic thing to say."

"You tell him, Cake Mix." Jakob, pleased, shot back a thanks before he could catch himself.

"It's Cupcake," she corrected. "That's what you call dumb girls. Not Cake Mix, Jakob." She laughed out loud. "You should stick to the way you're used to talking. I don't mind it. I'm used to it by now."

Sometimes you hear something that makes you happy for days.

At that moment they seemed to me two pups of the same litter, tumbling on the floor taking swipes at each other.

I suggested we sit up on the ridge in front of the Music Building and look back at the campus under the clear and star-filled sky.

Harry and Danny

I N the years since I left Paducah, I had called on Danny
twice. Both times he'd helped out. He could hardly do
otherwise; it was in his makeup. You had a claim on him,
he would honor it. Strangers could get annihilated by his
sudden bursts of temper, but not his friends.

The first time I called was five years after Ebie's death.
I was working for the Park Service in the Chisos Basin of
Big Bend National Park. (A few years later some student
discovered out there the remains of the wing bones of an
extinct flying reptile, a pterosaur, thought to be the largest
flying creature ever to inhabit the earth, a wing span of
fifty feet. At that time I wouldn't have been the one to find
him if he'd been spread out on the sandstone under my feet.
I wasn't looking to make discoveries. What I craved was
what I'd been hired for: to show how the sunset could be
seen between these two ridges at just this time of day, and
would be back again tomorrow.)

The reason that I hollered for Danny was that my father
had gone for good. He'd headed for his adopted homeland,
to open an *iskatola*, which means school, in order to teach
the dying Basques their dying language. What had precipi-
tated at last his exodus was something called the Burgos

Trial: a longtime Spanish torturer was killed on his own doorstep; random Basques were martyred in retaliation. For Wendell, this travesty constituted the last straw. At fifty-five he departed, to give the remainder of his life to his borrowed people.

I made the trip to tell him goodbye. He'd grown a full and unexpectedly red beard, which, below his dark hair and eyes, gave him a certain revolutionary flair. "My place is there," he told me, as if his place had ever been elsewhere. He was at his desk, where he stayed for the two days of my visit.

I was twenty-five.

Danny pulled himself loose from his work—he was back in Los Alamos then, and happy to be there—and went with me to Mexico City. He'd never seen it and wanted to. Louise was working two shifts and he said she was glad to get him out of her hair. They were a different pair.

It was stupidity, that trip. I wanted to go to Spain and drink with my father's oppressors and couldn't afford the fare. Mexico was a substitute: at least, all up and down the streets, four abreast, they chanted the language which was wiping out my father's kin. It was dumb; but so are most ceremonies of grief.

We saw Catholic cathedrals built on top of Aztec temples on top of Toltec sacrificial altars: nothing lasts. You could see the layers all over the marshy island that is Mexico City, because on every block they'd gouged out holes for the foundations of new buildings, foundations that looked like hay and rags and wires gummed together by some crew of giant toddlers. It was amazing comfort in its way: one culture simply buried another underfoot, all in good time.

(Are you listening, Wendell James? Spain will build a temple on your back.)

"You were a great help to me, Harry," Danny reminisced. "That was a bad time, losing Ebie. Not that I didn't see it coming. It was a Grade A catastrophe every time she went back to that swamp and those lunatics."

"You seem happy enough." It still stung that he had married Louise a scant four months later.

"Louise is a good woman. Strong. A lot like my mother."

He did not even entertain guilt. I could never induce it. (Which may have been his fascination for me, that being the one staple served up by the Roses K. in lieu of food at my house.) He didn't even seem to wonder if Louise might have hard feelings about being second after twenty years.

I envied him that.

In Mexico City I worked the conversation around to telling him that my name wasn't Roncevaux anymore; pretending that when my father left I'd taken my mother's maiden name, James.

"Harry James was a horn player," he informed me, which was another reason I liked Danny. "That'll make it easy to remember. But didn't you quit the fiddle yourself?"

"I did. I'm with the Park Service."

He went right ahead with his own train of thought. "It was a comfort to Ebie, having you play that time. It got her back to the piano herself. She could make music come out of that box the way I never heard it before or since. Not even my mother, who played by ear."

"She did. She was the best." I didn't ask about the nine-foot grand. I didn't want to hear if Louise was using it for a planter.

"How're you liking your job, then? You get along in the outdoors, don't you? I recall that. I tried it myself, to humor my old daddy, but I never took to it. You grow up in the coal country, you don't get much out of just looking."

"I like it. I like leaving a place the way I find it. My idea of a good life would be to move through the world like an Indian, not altering a twig."

We were in a fancy restaurant, called Rivoli, having had French chicken and house salad and a bottle of wine for me and a few glasses of whiskey for him. The dinner was too expensive, but it was close to our hotel and we had walked around the Zocalo at night while the pigeons and tourists slept. To me, who had never been there, the square looked like Rome; to Danny, who had, it looked like the Missouri State Capitol.

"The reason you're mad at your dad is he's a quitter." He set out this theory in answer to my problem over a fresh round apiece.

That made me see red. It seemed to me nothing could have been less true. Of all the accusations you could level at Wendell James, that was the most off the mark. I flared up. "Whatever you want to say about my old man, the one thing you have to say is that once he gets an idea he never lets it go. He's been stuck on the Basques for as long as I can remember. You don't know what you're talking about."

"He was a grown man long as you can remember. Some little boy got it in his head to change what he was, go over to the other side. That's what you got the brunt of, him wanting to run away before you were even a gleam."

It put me on the defensive. "You didn't stay back there

in West Virginia yourself. What do you call running away from that? If you're calling someone a quitter."

"What'd I quit? Cheat Lake? Poorhouse Hill? Nothing says a man has to stay in a one-horse town hoeing rocks in his backyard all his life. But I didn't run out on who I was born. Danny John Wister is the same as he started out."

It got my back up, I don't know why. I ordered a glass of whiskey for myself.

"What you have to remember," Danny plugged away, not picking up where I was, "is that by the time they bring you into the world the ones you call your mother and dad have a long time ago changed from being who they were. And who they were and how they got that way and what they needed to run from or go after remains a mystery to you all your life. My guess is your dad was a quitter from something."

I wasn't going to take that. It was one thing for me to hate my father, but it was another for Danny to be sitting there passing judgment like he had a right. What is the difference, I asked him, with a good deal of heat, after another glass or two, between someone going off to Los Alamos from those black mountains and someone who might happen to decide to leave a bomb plant and go back to dig for coal? "What's the big difference?" I shouted. "Just because he felt like reversing the process?"

I got very drunk. I have no memory of leaving the Rivoli, which we must have owed a small fortune.

All I recall is Danny tucking me into bed, saying: "Not that it sometimes doesn't pay to quit; else, you don't watch out, you're puking all over the place."

It may be he baited me on purpose, to get it out, some

of the festering anger, but I was never sure. At any rate, that visit served me for another five years.

Then Rose K. mater moved in with me. She moved into my place and wouldn't budge. She had got deathly thin; then in the month of her sitdown strike at my place she gained thirty pounds and was on her way to deathly fat. She'd been working hard protesting potatoes in Idaho, and the trouble was it wasn't like the good old days. Potato pickers had no desire to walk three hundred miles in the heat to see anyone.

I called Danny from a pay phone: "Say you've got a job for me. Get me out of here. Do something."

Within the hour he phoned, a proper caller who identified himself with Parks and Recreation, saying there was an opening if I could come to New Mexico for an interview. He was so firm and positive that I found myself believing him, and agreed on the spot to leave in the morning.

"I'll starve," Marie, my mother, threatened.

"You're good for a month on what you've put on this week."

"You can't leave me here. Harry, you can't leave me like this."

But I could, and I did. Self-defense is what it was.

I drove all night, and she didn't starve: I know from Christmas pictures. She moved in with a woman poor by profession, with seven children, some her own, and they decided to try the migrants in California, where the weather was better.

Los Alamos looked like a corporate copy of the rich parts of Santa Fe: expensive adobe homes, tastefully landscaped yucca and century plants, redwood decks, and aquamarine swimming pools. Sitting on a tableland in the mountains of New Mexico, it had the air of an American way station on a desert planet.

As it was clear that all the excitement and discovery took place offstage, in the labs, the houses were left to serve the function of fancy motels, and Danny's was no exception. (My first thought, on walking through the door, was to wonder if he was looking for someone with a hotplate.)

Although I recognized a few pieces from his former life —the sideboard, the wooden kitchen table which now held dried sagebrush—the rest was slipcovered in a green-and-brown cactus print. But he seemed delighted with it all: he was back at the work he loved; he had his comforts at home. And Louise.

She hugged me at the door as if we'd been friends for years. "How in the world are you, Harry? We were only the other day talking about you."

She was taller than Danny of course, hefty, with bottle-blond hair, leathery tan, vise-like handshake, and a brisk, warm way of moving things along. I got the idea that if you'd been her charge in the hospital she'd have had you out of there the next day, one way or the other, well or dead. Let's clear this bed out, girls.

She explained why she wasn't about to quit her job even though she didn't need to be working. "My old man used to answer the door in his undershorts. 'Go put on your clothes,' my old lady would shriek. 'It's my house,' he'd tell her, 'you pay the rent and buy the groceries and then you can tell me what I can and can't wear.' "

She saw my eyes take in the room and said right away in a firm voice: "We sent it to a state school, if you're after that grand piano. Somebody ought to get use out of it, I said, and I told Dan it'd be a sacrilege to take money for it."

She set out a box of Whitman's Sampler chocolates and a bottle of Henry McKenna bourbon. She was no cook, but she provided the basics. "You sent him to me," she said as she made us comfortable. "I'd have been waiting around in that Paducah, Kentucky, for another twenty years if you hadn't. We were just talking about you the other day, weren't we, Dan? Want coffee now? He said you might. I got instant and regular."

"I'm not sure I'm on your team," I said, to set the record straight. Her friendly reception had made me awkward.

"You sell yourself short, Harry. Dan told me you said to marry me, that I wasn't hanging around all those years for a man with no habits."

I had to laugh. I'd said that to Danny over the phone with a great deal of anger. That was the thing about him: ambiguities were wasted. Louise, it turned out, was much the same. She would not be put down. Nurses, I guess, can't waste time on subtleties.

She had her own version of Danny's congenital decency, and I found myself unable to dislike her after all.

"She doesn't seem to mind I'm here," I said to Danny when she'd retired.

"Louise don't mind anything. She goes her way. Besides, she has the early shift in the morning. She likes her nursing. That's the big concern with her. I would have married her in the beginning, but I had it in my mind to have kids."

"She didn't want to?"

"Wouldn't, couldn't, what's the difference? Back in those days she would have worked three full shifts a day if they'd let her."

In those days he had let Ebie move in. . . . But I didn't bring all that up. It was water, if not under the bridge, at least behind the dam as far as I was concerned.

"Your mom giving you trouble?" He settled down and got to the matter at hand.

I described her sitdown strike in my quarters at Big Bend.

"Some of them," he said, "have to be literally peeled off. You did right to call me. She doesn't have an audience, she'll take her show elsewhere. My old friend Threkeld had a mother like that, a real case of epoxy."

"She threatened to starve. . . ."

He studied me. "You ever hear from your old man?"

"Not lately." That was the truth. I hadn't heard from him earlier either. But Danny knew that. He was going through the formalities, being sociable. "Not since I saw you last."

"That was some time we had in Mexico City."

"Sorry."

"Nice place. Louise and I are going to fly down one of these days, when I can get her to take off. I told her about the square, said you said it looked like Rome."

"You thought it was the Missouri State Capitol."

"She's got her own mind."

Danny ate a chocolate cream, locating it on the Whitman's box-top chart to be sure, then dipping it in his whiskey. His barrel chest had become a barrel belly in the last five years. But, for the rest, he was unchanged. "There's worse events than nothing," he said. "Remember those lunatics in Louisiana kept Ebie chained in that house till she was nearly grown? That's worse than nothing. I always figured she set that fire, didn't you?"

"I never considered that."

"Don't let it get to you about your daddy is what I'm saying. There's worse events."

"Yeah. My mother moving in."

Over peanut butter for supper and cornflakes for breakfast all weekend, Danny and Louise urged me to stay on. But seeing the mountains, breathing deep enough to feel the altitude, had made me homesick for Aspen, which this was nothing like. I thought I should make the trip, as long as I was out that way, to see if time elapsed had changed either of us.

Which it definitely had.

My A-frame was now a hot-dog stand. The Epicure was filled with Design Research conferees. Everyone who could afford it ate lemon veal at the Golden Horn; only tourists went to the Copper Kettle, fixed price now $14.50. The Music School had abandoned the town completely and lived in its own world off the steep road to Maroon Bells, where racing cyclists practiced in the morning mist. Through the years enough human gliders had hit live wires to guarantee an avid audience every afternoon as the bird-men launched their flights.

The concert-goers now occupied lavish summer homes on Red Mountain, which they opened après concert. All the men were named Charlie and wore custom T-shirts and custom denims and had beautiful wives, if only for window-dressing. Each claimed to be just about to sleep with Liv Ullmann or Brooke Hayward, and each formed part of a claque for one or the other, but not both, of the stars of the new summer: violinists Itzhak Perlman and Pinchas Zukerman.

The coterie of ladies with philandering philanthropist husbands, who fancied me a likeness to their grandsons, had all passed on—wherever quality goes when it departs. In their place were crones who recounted over gin the ailments of their spouses: "His blood pressure is up again. His appetite is down. He hasn't been well for a long time. It may go on for years. The doctors have no idea."

A fretful descant which went well with the musicians and their swelling, drying instruments.

I went to hear Perlman and Zukerman—out of envy at how good they were, loss that I had never and would never play that well, and confirmation that even the best were the same: finding the bodies they'd been housed in infinitely inferior to those aged and fitted by such masters as Guarnieri and Stradivari.

I also went to a performance of Kodály's "Dances from Galanta" and noted that the composer had died two years after my summer in paradise. For that performance I sat outside in the grass with the young nursing mothers and backpackers and their sweet-faced Huskies who were allowed to listen tentside in the late afternoon shadows to the swelling sounds of concert from within.

The crowd on the fringes made me homesick. Not for my violin, nor for Ebie and Danny, but for Harrod Roncevaux—and nineteen.

The next morning I went to Ute Trail, with a stale roll in my pocket and a whistle on my lips. I called out, the old sound, half-whinney, and she came. Out from the path beside what was now a fancy condo complex came this half-blind, decrepit old yellow dog. "Hey," I said, "it's me. Want to take a walk?"

She wagged her mangy tail and led the way to the start of the trail, now obscured by a tangle of shrubs. About ten yards into it, I saw that she would never make it. There was only one thing to do; it was owed. Out of shape, without any wind, barely acclimatized, I picked up the old dog and carried her up all the switchbacks, gasping until I thought my chest would bust open. The last ten minutes, where the climb goes straight, I saw sheets of wavy red. But when we were on top, sitting flank by flank, and I had wedged her against my legs for safety, and she'd lapped at the water I poured in my hand, we settled down and I told her all that had happened in the years since we were pups. She did the same; and we shed a tear for old times and she gummed at the last of the stale roll. Then, when we were caught up, and I could breathe, and the red haze had subsided to a sunset, I carried her back down.

So here I was, five years later, my usual span of time for being able to make it on my own, dialing Danny again.

"I'm sure it's her, your daughter."

"She's dead. Twenty-seven years ago. You been drinking or something?"

"Ebie's. Paducah."

He cleared his throat. "That's a long time ago."

"You have to come."

Silence. Then, "It's not my business, Harry. She wasn't mine to begin with, I figured. I wouldn't know her if I saw her today standing right here. No point in stirring up muddy waters." He changed the subject. "Come out for a visit. You need to get away for a spell. You're hallucinating. Louise and I were talking about you the other day. We may be moving to Texas, it turns out. They made me an offer to work on a failed fusion contraption that's hard to resist."

"I want you to come, Danny. For me."

"Why didn't you say so?"

"Just see her. Don't talk to her, don't do anything. Just see her. Then you can go back. I'll pay."

"Doesn't seem much point to all that." He paused, then, after a few seconds: "I'll see what I can do."

"Come for the recital Friday night. See the woods up here. It's beautiful country; I'm running nature tours."

He hesitated. "What makes you think she's Ebie's?"

"Same birthday, same town."

"Must be a hundred of those."

"Three hundred and fifty."

"You know what you're doing?"

"Probably not."

"It may be a long trip for nothing."

"Tell Louise hello."

"We were just talking about you."

Harry on Us All

———◆———

"I ' M leaving if he comes."

"You're not leaving; your class gives final readings Saturday."

Jakob Plover lay face down on his bed. A position he had been in now for two hours since my call to Danny.

"Pretend he's my father."

"That's probably what you did when—" Muffled sobs.

"We never did, I've told you. Jakob—" I sat gingerly on the side of the bed. A hand shoved me away but he didn't turn his face.

"That's what you had in mind all along, since I told you. I wish I'd never told you. I should have torn up her bio the instant I read it. Miss Cake Mix. It's been nothing but trouble."

I picked my words carefully. My earlier attempts at explanation had not been too successful. I'd hurt him in spite of my intentions. "It's a matter of loss. I think those of us who go into conservation have had too much loss. We want to hang on to something: we collect family trees, or Queen Anne chairs, or bits of wilderness, or whooping cranes . . ."

192

At that he bolted upright on the bed and screamed in my face: "Don't you use that word to me! What do you know about conservationists? You come-lately mountain climber! My family has been conserving it since they hauled it over here on the first boat to come. They haven't let one stick or acre of it go. The first word I heard was Conservancy, the way other kids hear milk or Holy Bible. I could have been lying bleeding to death in the street and if it was a choice between saving me or saving one *fagus grandifolia*—" He sniffled, his teeth clenched.

I laughed. "One what?"

"See? See, you don't know any of that stuff. You just fake it. It's a beech tree, for your information, American beech. But that's not the big one, the big one we have to conserve is the *tsuga cannadensis*, which is your hemlock, in case you never knew. I think the Bay Colonists brought the seeds over pinned inside their shorts, and after they'd survived the first winter, those who didn't croak from the sight of all those Indians they were burning up in their wigwams, they planted those seeds so their descendants would have something to do. 'What shall we provide, brethren, for our Anglo-Saxon heirs who'll be tired in time of naming their kids after us and counting the money their money makes? Let's plant these and by the time they're three hundred and fifty years old it'll keep our great-great-great-grandkids busy building conserves to save the mighty hemlocks in.' "

"I didn't know all that. You never told me."

"Why do you think I never went on your dumb nature walks? Didn't that ever occur to you as odd?"

"The same reason I didn't go to your class; so as not to scare off the natives."

"Because I couldn't stand it if you were serious about that stuff. I've lived a whole month with your goddamn tree books right here on the table."

"What has this got to do with Danny?"

"I hate you, that's what. I bet I'd have liked your old man a whole lot: somebody who cared what happened to people and said the hell with all this fake shit around here."

"Maybe we were switched as infants."

"Not funny. Not that my folks aren't decrepit enough to be your parents, even."

"Bracket creep is aging." I retreated to a chair. I'd been quitting smoking all month, but this was time for a relapse. I dug a hidden pack out of my sock drawer. They tasted faintly of dirty socks, but then my socks had been smelling of tobacco. Maybe I could taper off by chewing on a crew sock when the craving got too much. I presented this line of reasoning to Jakob, but that was the last straw.

"You might remember 'spring is sweeter than winter,'" he flung at me. "Not that you ever read anything."

"Hard to argue, here in Vermont."

"I mean he's an *old man*." He went into the shower to drown his sorrows.

We obviously had one hell of a hot-water heater.

Jakob didn't have the foggiest idea why I wanted Danny to come; neither did Danny.

Jesus, why couldn't they understand? Danny had lost people right and left, a little girl just getting old enough to pee in an ice puddle on a hardwood floor. Jesus. And his old daddy, helpless and senseless at the end. And a wife that once he couldn't let out of his sight or take his hands off of. Why couldn't they see?

I wanted a place where each bee and wasp mattered,

each fern and web. Where nothing was lost, no footfall, no birdcall. They could all laugh at that: my folks, who wanted to overthrow it, change it, raze it, abolish it; Jakob, who'd had (but how was I to know?) a bellyful of playing second fiddle to a stand of trees; Danny.

What I wanted was for Danny to hear what I heard when she played, that and nothing more. (Unless to thank me for letting him have something from the past to keep.)

That's when I called him, after I heard her play.

That took place in a roundabout way. The music teacher and I were on minimally friendly terms. Her name was Fegg. She had a first name, but that had got dropped when it was learned that her assistant was a young man named Newton. Naturally, they were christened FigNewton by the first wag to put it together, and it stuck. The Fig-Newtons actually ran a lovely, easy, amazingly good show, for musicians. They had fewer takers than dance, theatre, or writing, and they knew it; so they agreed to fill the blank spaces, teach private or group, organize ensembles or duets, have recitals and extemporaneous sessions, anything. The result of which was, in the end, most of the students took a little music and some ended up taking a lot. I admired the FigN's for it. I knew musicians: such laissez-faire did not come easily.

Fegg was a type I'd known four hundred of before: long hair, bony face, big bottom, intense and voluble, wearing clothes that appeared to be discarded drapes. Newton was her complement: pudgy, eager, with square-cut fingernails, bouffant hair and Coke-bottom glasses. The kids liked to think that they were lovers. I knew better. The FigN's were simply variations on a theme.

At any rate, one day at lunch Fegg stopped off to speak

to us. "You should hear your *protégée* play," she said to me, giving the word the same emphasis Jeanetta did to *friend*.

"See what she thinks?" Jakob said after she left. "I told you."

I smiled at him; he would have been jealous of my shoes if I'd shined them twice a day.

"I might do that," I had answered Fegg. "Is she good?"

"Amazing. Her solo is the last number of the recital. She does a cut-down version of an arrangement of 'Prelude à l'Après-midi d'un Faune.' " She rolled her French artfully. "She has no finesse. Bad teacher. Atrocious teacher. But it comes out anyway. I intend to make arrangements for her to get proper instruction when she returns home. I forget where she's from. I plan to talk to her parents at the closing ceremonies, I understand they plan to come. I'm sure they will want to make proper provisions."

Jakob made a face. "The last thing Jelloville wants is talent, Fegg. You forget yourself."

She eyed him distastefully. "I don't think they should let college students assist with the program here. Even we wouldn't permit that, and musical talent matures early."

"Did you? I hadn't noticed." Jakob stared at her drapery.

"Truce," I pleaded. "I'll come hear."

I asked Jeanetta if she would mind if I came to her rehearsal.

She answered in her usual way. "This isn't for credit or anything, what we do up here."

I waited. I'd learned not to ask again, but to wait.

After a few steps she said: "I'm only playing to practice for the Deafs."

"I'll come watch, then; I won't listen."

"That's all right, Harry, if you do."

A lot of resistance still rides in me, going to a rehearsal. I haven't played in a . . . long time. And won't again. But I remember how it felt, against my chin, in my fingers. That was my trouble: I played my body.

I only went to hear Jeanetta because, truthfully, I wasn't expecting music. The FigNewtons wanted their final show to be the cream of the cream, surpassing the writers' writings, the dancers' dances, the players' play. I went to furnish a preliminary audience.

At any rate, when Jeanetta got up—and seeing her rise on those stubby legs hit me every time in the pit of my stomach—and walked over to the piano, a lovely grand looking like a harp laid on its side, as they do, and swiveled the stool until she almost had to climb to sit on it, and messed around with her sheet music for too long, seeming distracted, inattentive, I looked over at Fegg. Expecting to see her having a fit, which she wasn't. The fact that she sat, smiling, with her hands folded, should have told me something.

Then the girl began to play the prelude. At the start such a crashing sweetness, such brash, straight-out sweetness that you ached at hearing it, no subtlety, no timidity, and then, as the sharps shifted to flats—the dreamer wakes, to nothing—a crashing, banging rage took over. Each note pounded out as if encountered at just that instant, the hammers driven against strings until it became a fury that in the end subsided into a roar, a loud, wounded roar. I had heard the Debussy piece performed a hundred times at least; but I had never heard its soul before.

This was not Ebie's talent; rather, it was Danny, turning up the volume louder and louder, trying to absorb through simple vibration what he could not comprehend any other way.

I was weak when she got up. The silence after her sounded to me like chalk grating on a blackboard. I went up and hugged her—God knows what Fegg made of that, or, for that matter, what Newton made of it and passed on to Jakob. The hell with all of them is what I thought. She was connected to me, I had found her, and the rest of them could be damned.

"It isn't like school, you don't get a grade or anything," she said happily, glad to see me there. "So it was all right for you to come." She swiveled the stool back down and stood there as usual, Jeanetta Edna Mayfield in her pink shirt and yellow shorts, smiling as if everything was normal.

"I'll see you later, Harry," she said. "Tell your *friend* hello."

And she was off.

How could I not have called Danny?

"Where? Which one?" Jakob had, needless to say, come with me to meet Danny's train, wearing his Mark Kenelm Hopkins Williams II oxford shirt with rolled-up sleeves, tennis shoes, no socks, pleated cotton pants, and clean hair.

Danny got off, cheerful as if he had just got up, as if he took cross-countries every day for the heck of it.

"That runt?" Jakob said. "That fat runt?"

"Pretend he's your father. Rude day laborer, remember? It takes its toll, coming over on that boat from East Europe."

"I don't get it at all, if that's him."

"How come?"

"It's a waste of time is what. Your time. You want something to happen when Miss Cherry Jello collides with him, and nothing is going to happen, that's what. I don't get it, if that's him."

It was. I introduced them. Danny was pleased to meet Jakob and said that Louise sent her regards and that he could use a stiff drink.

We stopped on the way to Bennington at a roadside place where he could order a beer. Jakob asked for a glass of water without ice and a slice of lemon. That show of class was wasted on Danny, who went right on making conversation about how he had enjoyed the flight into New York and the train out, and that it was good to see this part of the country, and was this where I was living now?

Jakob had asked me if Danny "knew" about us. To tell the truth, I hadn't the foggiest idea what Danny thought about my love life, if he did. I had a hard enough time telling what he thought about his own. I had the feeling I could have said, "This is my lover," and he would have told me about this dog, or teacher, or football buddy that he'd once had, relating not so much to my words as to something in his own life that he could fit it to.

To tell the truth, I imagine he didn't think anything, but was glad, as he said, to make Jakob's acquaintance.

For a while I thought Jakob was going to have to ask him if he wanted to make something out of us being *fagus grandifolias*, but in the end he didn't.

I was having a hard time, sitting around having a beer, for thinking about the recital, and what was going to come from it. Jakob had been warned that if he so much as twitched a hair to show who Jeanetta really was, I would not only never speak to him again, but I would personally call his parents and tell them that he loved them a lot and wanted to graduate U. VA. and go into the family business.

"So what's he coming all the way up here for, if you're not going to point her out, for Christ's sake? It's a guessing game, and if he loses—and how could he not? she wouldn't stand out in a crowd of two—then it's back on the train and plane and home and that's it. I mean, aren't you going to tell him? Are you going to tell Mr. and Mrs. Insurance Salesman when they come? If you ask me, the end of Camp is the start of *camp*, if you ask me."

Jeanetta had told me that she had asked her mom and daddy to come up Saturday to hear her reading, and to have the nature cookout, and to watch her friends in dance, and see the play after the brunch on Sunday. But that she hadn't mentioned the music recital on Friday night. "I didn't lie," she said.

"You don't want them to hear you."

She had trudged along our path. "They've heard me play. A long time ago. I don't keep secrets from them, but they don't happen to know that I'm playing again, because I don't practice at home or anything, and I'm doing it for the Deafs is all. . . ."

"You don't want them to hear." I forgot and said it again.

"Is that awful, do you think?"

"No. Parents can take things away from you simply by perceiving them."

"You always talk like you didn't like your mom and dad at all."

"You always talk like yours never made a mistake in their lives."

She made a small smile. Not a large one, but a little one. I saw it as a crack in the dike.

"When you played the violin, did yours come listen?"

"Absolutely. They never missed a performance."

She looked pleased that she knew I was kidding.

That was Thursday, and we had been draggy on our walk. Thursday afternoon at the last of the session meant mostly rehearsals, as did Thursday night. The final program had to justify hiring all the resident artists, as well as make sure that word of mouth got a crop of students for the next summer.

"What did you do when you lived in Paducah?" she asked. We sat looking back at the campus from our perch near the Music Building. I could hear a flute duet. It was windy and warm, the day as well as the duet.

"Once, after I left the people I was visiting, I stopped for a couple of nights at Penyrile State Park. There was a lake, and I swam across, about a mile, and nearly froze to death. It was a lovely place and I was in the dumps at that time, so I swam and froze and walked in the pine trees. I remember that; they smelled wonderful."

"We call it Dawson Springs—lots of people go there in the summer, but not as many as to Kentucky Lake or something."

"I'd like to go back."

"And swim there?"

"See the park."

"You wouldn't be too far from Paducah."

"That's true."

She turned in my direction. "I got mirrors all around my room for my birthday, did I tell you that?"

"Is that what you wanted?"

"I used to look in them a lot." She seemed to be wanting to say something more.

The park idea was growing in my head. Park services

201

were everywhere. The pines had been beautiful. I wondered how that would work. The Mayfields might not see my visiting their daughter in its proper light. Almost everything I had going for me was going to work against me.

"You could come see the mirrors," she offered.

"I could."

"You could meet my mom and daddy on Saturday up here, and then they would already know you. If they knew you already—I mean, knew that you were the naturalist at Bennington—then, if you came, they'd already know you." She must have been thinking along the same lines that I was.

Which reminded me, I had to make a cover story for Danny. "I may not get to hear you again Friday night myself."

"That's all right." She looked disappointed.

"This old friend of mine is coming up to this neck of the woods, so we're meeting his train and bringing him out for the night. If he's tired, which he may well be, we're going to blow off the stuff here and take him out for a meal somewhere." I wanted to establish in her mind that there was no connection between her playing and my showing up with someone strange. My idea was to suggest that we probably wouldn't make it, and then if we appeared I could say that Jakob thought we ought to put in an appearance.

"Is he an old *friend?* Is Jakob jealous?"

"Not like that. He did me a favor once; I owe him one." I let it go at that.

"You didn't answer my question," she shot back at me. She was getting the idea.

I smiled. "Yes, Jakob is jealous."

"It's hard to help."

"It's hard to help if you make it happen."

"I used to get jealous of my boyfriend David, and I wasn't even in love with him, not the way Leslie is with Jimmy."

"Why did you, then?"

She considered. "You are because even if you don't love the person, you may need them and not want to let them go."

"I've heard about that." I had this need to pull on her pink shirt, but restrained myself. It had something to do with my getting a lecture on loss from someone who never even knew what she never had, something like that.

"When would you come down if you did?"

"Maybe I'll get there for your birthday."

"Next year I can get my license."

The writing assistant spent an hour in the shower when he heard my idea about going to see the pine trees.

"I think you're out of your mind," he said, re-emerging red as a lobster. "Why don't you admit to yourself what it is—that you want him back, that you want to ingratiate yourself into his life again, that's what it is."

"Danny doesn't live in that neck of the woods."

"I'm not gullible enough, no matter what you think, to buy that it's *her*." He flung himself face down, with one eye on the clock, as he had to rehearse his class.

"You're a snob, Mark K.H.W. II."

"You're worse. You're totally without discrimination."

"Paducah is a stone's throw from U. VA.; I'll come up for college weekends."

"Don't be facetious. We don't let hicks in anyway." He bounded up. It was time.

"It was just an idea, Penyrile Park."

"It stinks if you ask me."

" 'Some of us are ruled by the nature of station and habit; some by action and passion.' "

"Where'd you get that crap? You never read a book in your life."

"Don't ask."

"Your old man."

"I'm afraid so."

"I give up on you, Harry." He put a clean yellow shirt on, and slammed the door on his way out.

By Friday night I was ready to give up on myself. To describe the case of nerves I got before the recital is impossible. It was the vicarious nature of it. If I'd been playing myself, even in Carnegie Hall, I'd have been calm by comparison. But it wasn't my piece. It wasn't my recital. He wasn't my father.

If you'd asked me what I really wanted, I'd have had to say: for her to stand, him to see her, them to hug and weep, and her to go off with him and live happily ever after on peanut butter and Whitman's Samplers.

At least some dumb idea like that was in my head. It didn't help that Danny had called Jakob Plover "Jake" three times by the time the program got under way.

I had B.O., halitosis, psoriasis, athlete's foot, and a bad case of nerves.

There were about thirty kids, boys and girls, sitting in a semicircle up front and to the left of the flat wood floor that served as stage. Two pianos, a box arrangement for drums, and music stands for string trios had been set up. It wasn't a real performance in that nobody was in fine dress and there were no stage lights in the old carriage house that served as recital hall, but the kids were all cleaned up, and the FigNewtons had done all they could to lend the proceedings a festive air.

Jeanetta was next to last on the program. A mixed chorus opened and closed the show, with violins, cellos, flutes, drums, and piano numbers in between, so, in other words, she was the final solo.

As the chorus did its opening number I was ready to wet my pants or throw up or something. I was sitting on the edge of my folding chair—geared for the moment when Jeanetta stood and started spiraling the piano stool—when Danny turned to me. Jakob, on my left, sat glaring straight ahead, pretending not to know either of us. The choral group was doing a little catch from Anonymous, Twelfth Century, when Danny said in my ear: "Ho, ho, there she is." His whisper could be heard two rows in all directions. "Isn't she a pretty thing? What a sight. Same hair and eyes. Imagine that."

He stared in delight and mistaken recognition at a tall, made-up girl in the front row of singers. As she sang in harmony, she tossed her dark, glossy hair.

I couldn't utter a word. Jakob cackled and got up and left.

Still, I told myself, when he sees Jeanetta. When he hears. He'll know.

The entire show he never took his eyes off the brunette with the pointed chin, flapping hair, and mascaraed eyes.

At intermission he said, "I'm glad you rang me up, Harry. To tell the truth, it was the missing piece, without my knowing it. It's set my mind at rest. You know, Ebie got cold feet is the way I figure it; thinking about that lunatic daddy of hers down there in the swamp, she got cold feet about raising it. I'd made up my mind that I'd never know what happened to that baby. I'm glad you rang me up."

He settled down to enjoy the finish of the show.

During Jeanetta's pounding, wrenching version of the awakening he watched the dark-haired singer smooth her hair and put on lip gloss, getting ready for the final choral number. Nothing when Jeanetta stood up to play. Nothing when she swung the stool. Nothing at all when she wrung the sound out of the strings and boards of the smooth, curved box.

As she bowed, to the stunned applause of students who had not heard her before, she looked at me and smiled, to show that she was pleased I got there after all, and that she saw that Jakob had left because of my other *friend*.

Tears stung my eyes until I had to clench them closed. Sometime in there, while she played and he looked in the wrong direction, all the stuff I had been holding together for fifteen years fell apart. It was the way you imagine you would feel if you'd been run over by a truck.

"Same eyes, even," Danny whispered as the chorus lined up for their last number. He graced me with a stage whisper: "It was a missing piece, I admit it. Louise offered to find out for me, back at the beginning, but I said: leave well enough alone. Then I got used to not thinking about it. But you set my mind at ease, Harry. Isn't she the likeness?"

I took him to the train alone.

"Thanks for coming," I said. "Give my regards to Louise. You did right to marry her. Take care. Let me hear. I'll be out that way again one of these days."

"You ever hear from your folks?" he asked, not getting the drift of the fact that Harry James was a robot beside him.

"My old man, no. I figure when they shipped Picasso's 'Guernica' back to its homeland at last, he was there, with a few flags and such, to see it hung in place, or maybe he'd already got the firing squad, which he went over there for. No. I haven't heard a word. Not in ten years. In English, anyway. If he writes in Euzkara they probably burn it at the post office, don't you think?"

"What about your mother? Wasn't she threatening to move in with you that time I acted the Park Service man?"

"She's working with unfair onions in Oregon, but it isn't like the old days."

I wondered if thirty-five-year-olds ever cried right out loud on the winding roads of rural Vermont.

"Don't say anything to that girl, will you, Harry? I know I can count on you. No point in stirring up waters. But I'm grateful you rang me up."

He gave me a fatherly embrace at the station, and set out for the next lap. Louise would want to hear from me.

For about an hour I thought I'd keep on going, maybe end up in Canada tracking geese patterns, or in Detroit learning to make cars. I didn't want to go back.

For sure Jakob was waiting to rub it in, but that wasn't the worst of it.

Worse than that was it felt as if she was waiting, the girl, to hear what Danny had said. I knew that wasn't true, but it felt that way.

What hurt was knowing that you never knew them and they never knew you. None of them, not the ones who had you or the ones you adopted, could pick you out of a crowd. They could pass you on the street and never know that you were theirs. Anybody else could be more kin: a yellow dog, blind and senile, could wait for years in case you ever decided to have another go at the switchbacks at her end of town.

It was half past three when I finally crawled back into the room.

Jakob had probably spent four hours in the shower, hoping I'd catch him there. He appeared waterlogged, but I didn't care. "Shut up," I said, before he could open his groggy mouth. "Don't say a word."

The next day, after his writers' readings, I met the Mayfields. "Sorry I didn't get to hear her read," I said. "I had car trouble last night, getting back from Albany. Bad roads, a lot of curves."

"That's all right," Jeanetta answered. "Jakob is Xeroxing our stories into a book for us."

"Good idea."

Betty Sharp Mayfield was glad to know me. "You've been important in Jeanetta's life, she tells me. This is certainly a fit place to talk about nature, if there ever was one. I never saw any place like this for beauty. We enjoyed the whole drive up; it was a vacation for both of us."

"Glad to know you, boy," Finis said. "She did good, didn't she? My JeanEddie?"

She did, I told him. "Will you be heading back home from here?"

"We thought we'd see New York City as long as we're up this way. That's one of the marvels of nature. It was that or Niagara Falls, and since we're already married. . . ." He chuckled.

"Jeanetta tells us you may be visiting in Kentucky." Betty had got caught up on what was going on.

"I've had, uh, this tentative offer from their parks department. I don't know yet. I'm involved in a Hudson River project at this time, but if I ended up there it would be good to have friends nearby. If that wouldn't impose on you folks—?"

"Not at all," Finis assured me. "Any friend of Jean-Eddie's is always welcome at our house."

They excused themselves then, because they wanted to meet the other teachers and make a start on loading the car.

"Thanks for helping to take care of my little girl," Finis said, and gave a firm handshake to seal it. " 'Till then light be the ashes upon thee and may the sunshine of even beam bright on thy waking.' "

"Now they know you," she said.

"You've got nice folks."

She was quiet. "Is Jakob still mad at you?"

"He'll get over it."

We were standing by the start of our walk, sleeping bullfrogs a few yards away.

There wasn't much time to say much. Or much to say.

I needed to go back fifteen years and start over.

What she needed was somewhat the same.

I thought of Fabre tending his bit of land, his Lettuces and Turnips, his Common Wasp and Mason Bee. It had a strong appeal.

"Maybe I'll get there next year for your birthday."

"That's all right, if you don't."

"Let me know how it goes with the Deafs."

"They don't mind whatever you do."

We stood around a minute more.

She asked: "Did you really know my daddy?"

"Yes," I said, tugging on her yellow shirt. "He was my daddy, too."

SHELBY HEARON was born and raised in Marion, Kentucky, but spent most of her adult life in Austin, Texas. Her six novels previous to *Afternoon of a Faun* are *Armadillo in the Grass*, *The Second Dune*, *Hannah's House*, *Now and Another Time*, *A Prince of a Fellow*, and, most recently, *Painted Dresses*. She has received a Guggenheim Fellowship, and has twice been the recipient of the Texas Institute of Letters Jesse Jones fiction award. She has taught at The University of Texas, Bennington College, and the University of Houston. The mother of a daughter and son, she now lives in Westchester County, New York, with her husband, philosopher Bill Lucas.